Cast in Time

Book 1: Baron

By Ed Nelson

Other books by Ed Nelson

The Richard Jackson Saga

Book 1: The Beginning

Book 2: Schooldays

Book 3: Hollywood

Book 4: In the Movies

Book 5: Star to Deckhand

Book 6: Surfing Dude

Book 7: Third Time is a Charm

Book 8: Oxford University

Book 9: Cold War

Book 10: Taking Care of Business

Book 11: Interesting Times

Book 12: Escape from Siberia

Book 13: Regicide

Book 14: What's Under, Down Under?

Book 15: The Lunar Kingdom

Book 16: First Steps

Stand Alone Stories

Ever and Always

Mary, Mary

Dedication

This book is dedicated to my wife, Carol, for her support and help as my first reader and editor.

With special thanks to Ole Rotorhead for his technical insights on how things really work.

Then there are my beta readers: Ole Rotorhead, Lonelydad, Antti Huotari, and Pat O'Dell.

And never forget the professional editor: Morgan Waddle.

Quotation

According to 'M' theory, ours is not the only universe. Instead, 'M' theory predicts that a great many universes were created out of nothing.

Stephen Hawking

Copyright © 2023

ISBN: 978-1-953395-71-9

Library of Congress Control Number: 2023912483

Table of Contents

Cast in Time...i

Other books by Ed Nelson..................ii

Dedication..iii

Quotation...iv

Copyright © 2023 v

Prologue 1

Chapter 1 12

Chapter 2 24

Chapter 3 34

Chapter 4 45

Chapter 5 58

Chapter 6 71

Chapter 7 81

Chapter 8 92

Chapter 9 104

Chapter 10 116

Chapter 11 127

Chapter 12 138

Chapter 14 153

Chapter 15 161

Chapter 16 172

Chapter 17 183

Chapter 18 195

Chapter 19 206

Chapter 20 218

Chapter 21 229

Chapter 22 240

Chapter 23 251

Chapter 24 263

Chapter 25 274

Chapter 26 285

Chapter 27 297

Chapter 28 308

Chapter 29 320

Chapter 30 331

Backmatter 342

Prologue

"Fire!"

My ten crossbowmen released their bolts upon my command. The hours of training paid off. All six of the charging knights' horses went down. The knights were trapped under their mounts or lay broken on the ground from the sudden deceleration.

My twenty-first-century tactics in this 8th century were saving my adopted people. These were more like fourteenth-century tactics, but who was counting?

What was I, Jim Fletcher, a farm boy from Ohio who had died at the age of ninety-two in 2010, doing in the body of a twenty-four-year-old Baron in 8th-century Cornwall?

I think it is Cornwall, but there are some differences from the Cornwall that Dory and I knew. Not differences in culture, that was to be expected, but geographical differences.

I had no idea why I was here.

The action continued as I mused about what was happening in front of me. Contrary to war leaders of the time, I did not stand on the front lines but commanded from the rear.

1

It wasn't far from the front, and I was protected from the main charge, able to command the entirety of my small army. Well, band. A small band.

My crossbowmen were trained to aim for the horses. Armor for horses wasn't yet in use.

Heck, this was before stirrups were in use! Even the knights' armor was rudimentary compared to later versions. The real Romans had better armor five hundred years ago.

Chain and plate mail was in the future. This armor was similar to bullet-resistant vests from my time. Flat pieces of metal in leather pockets.

Fifty yards behind the Knights were the attacking Baron's footmen. At the start of the battle, there were forty of them. Now some were running from the field as the Knights went down.

I had only twenty-five men to counter their Army. But at least they weren't running from the field.

Per the plan, the fastest ten of my footmen charged into the fallen Knights and finished the job with war hammers.

Shooting horses and using sledgehammers to beat people to death may not seem sporting, but this didn't pretend to be.

It was war, and I knew war all too well. From World War II to Vietnam I had been there. Now that I'm here, will I change history so much that those events never happen?

Once the horses and Knights were dead, they retreated. The horses were killed to put them out of their pain. The Knights were no longer a threat and demoralized the remaining footmen.

The action also raised the morale of my soldiers as the 8th-century equivalent of the main battle tank was taken out of the equation.

My footmen followed the crossbowmen who had retreated through the scattered caltrops. Small sticks with cloth marked three safe paths through the field.

If the footmen charged, they would have a nasty surprise with our medieval minefield.

Across the way, an enemy Sergeant, a soldier with a Knight's skills and tools but without a Knight's golden spurs, was trying to rally the remaining troops. He wasn't having much luck.

These weren't trained soldiers but conscripted farmers. Baron Wendon had counted on his Knights' charge breaking my forces. It was well known that my Barony had no Knights, so he was confident he could roll over us.

His so-called Army was armed with poor spears and billhooks. They were clustered as a rabble rather than in a soldierly formation.

My troops were only a step above them, but they were in a formation. Each of my people wore a green armband giving us a uniform appearance.

The enemy Sergeant had rallied his remaining troops and charged. We waited in place. Let them wear themselves out running up the moderate slope in front of us.

The slope could easily be walked, but it was wearing on running troops, especially since they were charged up on adrenalin. The crossbowmen fired once more just before the attackers hit the caltrop field.

Their fire took down five of the enemy by direct hits and another six by men stumbling into them. These men could get back up, but the momentum was broken.

These caltrops were not the six-inch ones for a horse but three inches for men. There were hundreds of them. Without hard-soled boots, the enemy footmen were disabled.

By the time the enemy had troops across the field, the crossbowmen had cranked their bows and shot another flight of bolts.

The crossbowmen retreated behind our footmen and started to crank their bows again. It wasn't needed. Our front line cut down the dozen enemy footmen who made it that far.

Prisoners were taken, and the wounded were treated as well as possible. These were now my people by right of conquest, so they must be cared for.

"Sergeant, detail men to retrieve the caltrops and collect the weapons. And detail two men to accompany me to loot the Knights," I said.

I had to loot the Knights in person, or I would see little of the loot. That was the nature of the beast in these days.

Not that there was much to loot. Baron Wendon had the most, but it was only a few silvers. I had to hope that his fortress had more. I had to act fast if I was going to add his Barony to mine.

My plan wasn't to conquer my neighbors, but if they gave me no choice, they would face the consequences.

I never doubted that my forces would win. It enabled me to march with my crossbowmen and fifteen footmen at once. We had a pack train of supplies ready to follow. Our scouts had marked our path.

Baron Wendon's castle was only ten miles from mine. Ten miles seemed a very short distance to me. But once I remembered that most people in this time never went more than five miles from their place of birth, it made sense.

The early morning battle allowed us to arrive at the Baron's castle in the late afternoon. While not impressive as a castle, it would have been a bear to attack if the gates in the ten-foot-high wall were closed.

Thankfully the gate was wide open. We were able to march right up to the castle and go inside. The Baron was so confident of victory that he hadn't left a guard at the gate.

There were a few old men with spears who surrendered immediately. They may seem primitive to my modern eyes, but they weren't stupid by any means.

The Baron had left his wife and two small children behind. I was left with a dilemma of what to do with them. The original Baron whose body I inhabited would have killed them with no remorse. It was the sensible thing to do in that day and age.

Letting the wife live was inviting immediate trouble as some of the remaining population would be loyal to her. The two children represented future problems.

The six-year-old boy would grow up thinking he had been robbed of his title. The four-year-old girl could be married to another Baron to secure an ally for the cheated young Baron.

The recent widow didn't seem upset about the death of her husband. She only seemed to care about her children.

I saw an opportunity in her attitude. While my men explored the Keep, she and I talked in their living quarters.

"You don't seem upset by your husband's death."

"He would beat me if I didn't please him."

"Where are you from?"

"My father is a merchant in Saltash. He wanted his grandchildren to be titled, so he paid Baron Wendon to marry me."

She and I talked for a while. I found her to have more education than I expected. When quizzed on this, she confessed that she had been taught to read and write as her father had no other children to follow him.

She ran the family chandler business when he had to go on trading ventures, obtaining tree limbs and trunks for sailing vessels.

The Wendon castle steward was one of those killed in the recent fight. I asked her if she could run the castle.

"I have been performing the Steward's duties for the last two years. He was drunk most of the time. He and my husband were seldom sober enough to keep order in the Keep. I had to order provisions, hear the people's complaints, and try to keep the place together."

She continued, "The former Baron learned you had no Knights, so he thought it would be an easy victory. He had enough brains left to realize that his Barony was falling apart. He thought if he conquered yours, there would be enough loot to continue to support this one."

Her apparent intelligence and lack of loyalty to her dead husband gave me an idea.

"I didn't set out to conquer this Barony. Could you continue to run it for your son if I recognized him as the rightful heir and declared him the Baron?"

I thought she would collapse when I asked this. The brave front she had been putting up dissolved. She thought she and her children were to be killed.

"I would leave one of my men to act as Steward, but you would be your son's regent until he is of age."

I went on, "There are changes I have made in my Barony that would benefit here."

Her eyes lit up as I described our new sanitation systems, education, and improved farming methods. My policy of not letting my people starve in times of famine.

While talking, I notice she is a handsome woman and has all her teeth. Having a full set of teeth was a rarity at the time. While decay from sugar wasn't present, basic gum care was a huge problem. There was nothing about her that a bath wouldn't cure.

It seemed we were at a crossroads about bathing. The Romans had their baths and used them frequently. Most conquered areas adopted the practice. They had influenced this Cornwall but hadn't conquered it to change its customs. At least in this reality. Pity.

"What do you want in return?" She asked.

"You and your son to swear allegiance to me and provide men if needed for war."

She had no reservations that I could see in doing this. It would allow her and her children to live.

9

Not only to live but to remain in power. Expecting death, she now faced life.

My men secured the small fortress and assembled its inhabitants. When the people of the castle and the immediate surrounding area were assembled, I explained the change in their circumstances.

The news was accepted with little reaction. The former Baron hadn't treated the people well, but he wasn't horrible to them either.

To them, it sounded like business as usual. That would change. The village headman was brought to me. I explained to him that there would be changes, but I wanted him to observe them in my village so he could explain them to his people.

You could tell he wasn't used to this treatment. Confusing him further, I asked that his wife accompany him to bring back a women's perspective on the coming changes.

I knew that when she saw the better lifestyle of my people, she would be our most avid supporter. The headman thought he ran his village, but I knew better.

The old Baron had less than five hundred silver in his treasury. This small amount wouldn't have supported the castle for very long. It explained why he decided to conquer me. I told the mother of the new Baron that I would send one thousand silver to support her son. This amount was to be considered a no-interest loan with no set repayment date.

To say she continued to be amazed would be putting it lightly. I would have taken her as a wife if she had been younger. She was the most attractive and intelligent woman I had met so far. She just needed a bath.

I arranged for ten men and a Sergeant to remain as my representatives. The Sergeant understood that The Lady of the castle was in charge. He was there to report any attempted treason.

I could only trust so far.

While arrangements were being made, I thought about how I had gotten here. Ironically it started on my deathbed.

Chapter 1

I was born James Douglas Fletcher on May 28, 1918, in Logan County, Ohio, to Paul Douglas Fletcher Junior and Janet Elizabeth Fletcher nee Rupert. Math never worked out for the marriage and birth dates, but there was a war.

I was an only child. Complications in childbirth prevented any other children.

Growing up on a small farm in Ohio gave me a taste of hard work and learning to be responsible for my actions. It took several painful trips to the woodshed, but by the time I was fourteen, I understood.

I still don't think it was my fault the explosion was that large when I lit off the methane gas in the pile of cow manure.

Not that I didn't do rebellious things. I just didn't get caught. I smoked an entire cigarette before deciding the taste was terrible and wanted no part of it. When I inhaled deeply, the smoke would tear my lungs apart.

If that were what it took to look older and more worldly, I would be happy to look young and naïve.

Beer was a different story. I loved the taste of it. I also quickly learned the price to be paid for drinking too much. Savoring the taste was better than chugging a bottle and having a hangover. One hangover was enough.

By the time I was sixteen, I had learned my way around a bra strap and other things. But the great mystery of life still evaded me.

My father, Paul, had served in the Great War and returned home a Major. While doing well in the Army, he had no desire to make it a career. Any career would have been limited because he was an ROTC callup.

Still, he had fond memories of the Army, at least when he wasn't in the trenches. Those times weren't talked about.

My grandfather Paul Douglas Fletcher Senior had been with Colonel Roosevelt and the Rough Riders on Kettle Hill. That day was his only real battle in the war and he would recount the events at the drop of a hat. I could recite the story along with him.

All in all, the experiences of my father and grandfather left me with a desire to be in the Army. I told my parents of my wish when I was in the ninth grade.

Dad told me if I was going to be in the Army, it was best to be an officer. To achieve that, I should go to West Point. To attend West Point, I needed good grades, participation in extracurricular activities, and political backing.

Later I learned my parents, in private conversation, thought this was a phase and that I would never meet all those goals.

In High School, I demonstrated a strength of character that I held for my entire life.

I went out for football and track and field, making both teams. Making the teams wasn't that impressive, considering the size of my rural high school.

I also joined the Chess Club because I truly loved to play, though I never got beyond expert ranking.

I tried out for several school plays but wasn't an actor. My lines came across as wooden at best. When not acting, I was considered a well-spoken young man and viewed as sincere by my peers. At least, that is how I interpreted it.

Academically I had an advantage that began to show in the ninth grade when classes became more difficult. I had a photographic memory. Giving me the advantage of every test being an open-book test.

The disadvantage was that it was like leafing through a textbook to find the answer. It took time. I couldn't take a test of one hundred and fifty questions and look them all up. I still had to pay attention and learn as much as I could.

Then in a test, I would only have to look up a few items. If there was enough time when I finished, I could go back and "look up" the correct answer if I was in doubt.

One would have thought I would have gotten 100% on everything, but human memory is funny. I would be certain I had the right answer and not look it up. Because of this, I only got 98% correct consistently, which still impressed my teachers.

I had to spend time on my work to understand it. Just because I could remember what the book said didn't mean I got it. I was considered an excellent student but not a genius.

It might be because my mind was frequently on the next bra strap.

My American History teacher was a graduate of West Point. He spoke of his experiences occasionally, so I felt free to share my desires. In return, I learned that my local Congressman made the appointments in our area.

Politics became the only bone of contention between Dad and me. Dad was a staunch Wilson Democrat and the Congressman, a Republican.

I signed onto the Congressman's campaigns, knocked on doors, waved signs at street corners, and helped set up rooms for fundraisers. By doing this, I became known to the Congressman.

As with all campaign events, there were fallow periods where I had a chance to explain my desire to attend West Point. While now a political appointment, it made it easy for the Congressman to favor me.

I received an appointment to attend the Military Academy at West Point upon graduation from High School. Assuming I succeeded in school, I would be in the graduating class of 1939.

While not the smartest person in the room, I was probably the hardest worker. The material I had to learn didn't need a genius. It just needed someone willing to do the work.

Work was what I was good at. I was like a bulldog in my studies. I wouldn't let go until I had mastered the material and completed my assignments.

My major was mechanical engineering. These courses started me on my lifelong love of Engineering in all its forms.

But I wasn't a recluse. I made friends with my classmates. When I was made a team leader on projects or field assignments, they followed me willingly.

One report by an instructor stated, "Students follow Cadet Fletcher because they know he will put in the work to complete the mission while taking care of his people."

I graduated seventh in my class of 456 cadets. That was out of over 700 of us who had started in the summer of 1935. Like many high-ranking students, I chose the Army Corps of Engineers as my first assignment following in the footsteps of such famous graduates as Robert E. Lee.

It would be best if you didn't think I was nothing but a grind in school. I gained fame when I won a bet that I could keep a pet in our barracks for one month without getting caught.

I had noticed a light bulb, enclosed in a globe, burned out in a closet. So I turned the globe into a fish tank. The goldfish lived for six weeks before I had to flush it. I was lucky my nickname didn't come from that event.

At five foot eleven inches and one hundred and forty pounds, I did come across as skinny and always eating my favorite snack. So, they called me Slim Jim.

After my graduation in 1939, I went on active duty. As a Second Lieutenant, I probably did every dumb thing a Butterbar could do. But by listening to my Sergeants, I survived the experience.

Once I realized that the officer above me would give me an order, I had to tell my Sergeants to make it happen. It was not a Second Lieutenant's job to think!

By the time I was a First Lieutenant, I was in North Africa, building tank traps and fortifications. It was here I received my first Bronze Star and Purple Heart.

By the war's end, I was a Major through battlefield promotions with two Bronze Stars and a Silver Star. I also had three Purple Hearts (none of which were serious wounds), plus various campaign medals, which made me look like a serious soldier. As I put it, I frequently forgot to duck but kept working anyway.

It did stick in my craw that we combat engineers couldn't wear the CIB.

After the war, I met a young lady at Fort Leonard Wood. After dating for a year, I married Dorris Davidson in 1948. It was the beginning of a partnership that lasted over fifty years. Our one regret was that we never had any children.

We considered adoption but didn't want to put our children through the continuous changes being an army brat would require. Instead, my officers and their wives became our children.

After World War II, I continued my engineering education, adding a degree in civil engineering. When Korea came along, I was back on the front lines.

This time I destroyed many bridges and then built them back up. Being a Major, I didn't spend as much time at the front under fire. At least that is what I told my wife in letters home.

It still had its moments. Enough moments to receive a second Silver Star, a Distinguished Service Cross, and another Purple Heart. How was I to know that the units I was supporting bugged out and the only thing holding the North Koreans back was my unit?

It was touch and go, but an artillery barrage saved the day. But it didn't happen until I had my unit dug in. Handy things, those bulldozers. I then proceeded to round up a short battalion of four hundred troops.

I dug them in and created a salient that stopped the North Korean advance long enough for troops to be brought back into line.

I was awarded the Distinguished Service Cross for my actions during the bug-out and another battlefield promotion to Lieutenant Colonel.

Unlike Patton, I wasn't observed when I decked the officer leading the bug out. That was later in a bar in Seoul. I chose my moment well when a bar fight had already started.

After Korea, I spent time with the Civil Engineering side of the Corps of Engineers. My units built dams and levees up and down the Mississippi for the most part. I continued my education in Engineering.

Dory, was the perfect military wife. She took the enlisted men's wives under her wing and helped with their problems, mostly by counseling and sometimes by direct intervention. Woe unto the soldier who mistreated his wife.

As I rose in rank, she grew in her poise. Now it was caring for wives of philandering Captains. Those that didn't learn quickly fell by the wayside.

She could chew out a Major and have tea with a General's wife equally at ease.

In 1958 I was promoted to full Colonel since I now had enough Time in Grade and Time in Service.

When Vietnam came along, I was given my first star. I was in charge of all engineering projects in Viet Nam. Now I was constructing airstrips, firebases, bridges, digging wells, and anything else the Brass could think of.

I didn't get out into the field very much anymore and didn't care. I was getting too old for that shit. Also, the troops in this war differed from the other two I had been in. Earlier wars had a sense of patriotism about them.

While many in the earlier wars waited to be drafted, it wasn't a cause for resentment. All were in the draft.

These soldiers felt that only the lower classes were being sent to war. These men were unwilling draftees. The level of frustration was high.

There was no real sense of purpose. On the occasions I got out in the field and talked to the people on the sharp end, it seemed like the Brass back in Saigon had no idea what was happening.

It was good that the Army had sent me to General Officer training, or as they called it, "Charm School." Its purpose was to teach me how to deal diplomatically with foreign governments, especially their military. Also, our congress and high-ranking officers of sister services.

I privately thought it taught me how to say nothing, lie my ass off, and smile while doing it.

In 1970 I was promoted to Lieutenant General and Commanding Officer of the US Army Corps of Engineers and given the traditional set of "Gold Castle" insignia passed down from General Douglas MacArthur.

I surrendered them in turn when I reached the forced retirement age of fifty-five in 1973.

Since I was in a specialized branch of the Army, I was never under consideration for a fourth star. That was fine by me. Getting my third took more political posturing than I had the stomach for.

The only regret I had about all the awards I had been given was that I wasn't eligible for the Combat Infantry Badge. I had been under direct fire for days in three different wars. If they were shooting at you and you were shooting back, that should be enough to earn the award.

During my tenure in the Army, I never quit my schooling. I have a Ph. D. in Mechanical Engineering and a master's in civil engineering. I had so many minors I had to make a list.

I was now about to start another phase of my life.

A life-changing phase.

Chapter 2

Upon retirement, we moved to Florida and started the retirement lifestyle. Golf outings, fishing, movies, and dinner with new friends.

That lasted about six months. Dory and I hated it. We were used to keeping busy. Doing nothing wasn't for us. We weren't being fair in our thinking to those who were happy with that life, but it just wasn't us.

Finances weren't a problem. My Army retirement, plus our savings, and stock investments left us comfortable.

I had bought stock in technology companies like IBM and AT&T. My wife likes what she calls people companies such as Coca-Cola and the new hamburger chain, McDonald's.

We hemmed and hawed around for months, checking things out. Then eventually decided to join the Peace Corps.

The initial training was interesting. It covered technical areas such as linguistics, cross-cultural, health, safety, and security.

As far as technical, health, and safety plus security, they immediately wanted me to stay in the US as an instructor.

But we wanted to go out into the field, so I declined. Linguistic training was a slog, but I got through it. Dory flew through it. What surprised me the most was the cross-cultural training.

It wasn't the African culture that gave me a problem. The program was based on comparing African ways with American ways.

I didn't have a problem with the African ways. After serving on three continents and many countries, I expected them to be different. It was what I learned about American culture that was amazing.

The culture of the American military is different than that of mainstream America.

It turned out that I had visited America but hadn't lived in it. First of all, the Army is a male culture. Yes, there are women in the Army, but don't kid yourself, it is a male culture. It is a physically fit culture. We cull the weaklings.

A culture of order and slow change. As an Officer, I was used to giving orders and not having to coax people.

When I needed resources for a job, I requisitioned them. In the Army, I decided how or if entire programs would be supported at my retirement rank.

Now I was expected to beg, borrow, or steal what was needed.

When we finally got in-country after our three-month training, we had more lessons to learn. The Peace Corps expected us to live with host families. In some cases, this meant sleeping on the couch.

Since we had private funds, we rented a grass shack of our own. We would eat meals with our hosts or even invite them to our place for dinner.

There were other Peace Corps Volunteers (PCV) in our area. We were by far the oldest. Most were in their early twenties.

Dory soon became the den-mother. I was treated as a senior officer, like in our old life.

The locals drove me nuts.

I would work on a project to improve their farming methods, and they would sit under a tree all day. They knew that free food would be shipped to them by the many Non-Governmental Organizations (NGOs), so why bother to work?

I couldn't convince them that the NGOs might not be around forever or that PCV people like me would not be available to teach in the future.

Dory and her cadre of female PCV workers were more successful with cleanliness and sanitation. The idea of not losing so many babies appealed to the local women. The men didn't seem to care. They could always make more.

So instead of improving farming methods, we worked on a clean water supply and a sanitation system.

I'm not talking about running water in the house or an indoor privy. We ran PVC pipe from a fast-running stream to a filtration bed, then pumped it to a water tank by hand. From the tank, water could be obtained from one of several water faucets installed below the tank.

This setup gave a reliable water supply to the small village. Before installing this setup, the village women would haul buckets of water from the nearest stream.

The easiest place at the stream was downstream from where their few cattle grazed. The cows would go into the stream to cool off and, of course, poop in the water.

I even saw a couple of the boys herding the cows do it the same way.

It worked fine until the water tank was empty. No one wanted to spend time or energy pumping it.

We also built a communal privy with separate men's and women's sides.

It required a lot of digging by the PCV and pipe laying, but we had water from above the water supply running through the privy and returning it to the fast-running stream far below the water supply.

It worked fine until it stopped up. It seemed the privy was a good place to dump any unwanted items.

We had made it possible through a small door to go down and unblock it. After my third trip, I refused to go anymore. Other PCV felt the same.

To obtain the building materials, we had to trade and barter. The Peace Corps only lent people. The local government and NGOs had to come up with money or the materials needed.

The NGOs were mostly church groups, and I finally got tired of having to attend their services in trade for the materials. Near the end, they even required me to bring so many locals to their events so they could try to convert them.

The few locals I could convince to come were teenage boys who only wanted to ogle the white girls there. I didn't care about the race issue. It was the cultural differences that could cause problems.

I finally just started paying for the materials out of pocket. After two years of backbreaking labor, we had a water system that wasn't used because no one wanted to pump water and a blocked-up sewer system.

Despite requests and even a little pressure, Dory and I decided the Peace Corps wasn't for us. When we got home, I made another discovery.

The Peace Corps would occasionally send camera crews around to film our work-in-progress. Most pictures were staged with other volunteers directing smiling natives.

The natives were smiling because the Peace Corps paid them an extortionate rate to work that day.

I saw the result one evening of a PSA being run on late-night TV. They were recruiting for the Peace Corps and using retired Lt. General James Fletcher as a role model.

To say I was upset would be putting it mildly.

When interviewed on a local TV station, I was asked about my African experience.

"When I was young, I learned the saying, 'You can lead a horse to water, but can't make him drink,' They proved it is true.

"If you are disillusioned with your Peace Corps work, why are you allowing them to use you in their ads?" The interviewer asked.

"I was never asked. I hadn't read my contract close enough to know the Corp didn't need my permission."

"So, will you and your wife be going back?"

"We are done. It isn't the Peace Corps people who are the problem. It is those that won't help themselves."

The Peace Corps had been trying to get me to sign for another two years. After that interview, they quit calling.

Dory and I were now back to where we had started. We were both fifty-eight years old and had to figure out what to do.

While waiting for something to come up, I took more Engineering courses at a local college. I was halfway through my first semester when it hit me.

I would become a professional student. Why not spend my time doing something I love? I applied to several of the major engineering schools. All of them accepted me.

I chose MIT, where I would be a student for the next thirty years. We bought a house within walking distance of campus. Dory joined several women's groups and was always on the go.

I earned PhDs in Mechanical, Civil, and Geo-Technical and a master's in chemical and electrical Engineering.

I majored in manufacturing, material science, transport, optical, and mining metallurgical.

I had minors in aerospace, thermal, paper, agricultural processes, structural, water resources, architecture, power, electrical, petroleum, geological, and ceramics.

It sounds like a lot, but I didn't have to repeat the prerequisite courses. So, it wasn't a heavy load, just consistent year after year.

I was written up in many journals as the most educated engineer in the world. I tried to remind everyone that I had practical experience in the Army, but I should be considered a new grad for everything else. Full of book learning but no use until I gained field experience.

I enjoyed learning for the sake of learning. It was much better than having some son of a bitch trying to kill you. The young reporters didn't get that either.

By the time I was eighty-eight, I had enough trouble getting around that I had to quit school. MIT surprised me by throwing a going-away party. They also presented me with an honorary degree as a Ph.D. in professional studenting.

All in good fun. I was sad as I knew this was my last run in life.

Dory's health had deteriorated, and she had to be put in a nursing home. I visited her every day for two years until I showed up one morning, and they told me she had passed an hour before I got there.

Soon after, my health went downhill; I blamed it on a broken heart. I was admitted to a facility and lived there for my last two years.

One evening I relived my life almost scene by scene and realized it was time.

My wife and I were never religious. That said, I had formed an idea of death. Not heaven or hell, or even a limbo. A fade to black and you were gone, never to wake again.

I knew I was dying, my body had started shutting down. The one symptom that I didn't exhibit was confusion. I knew what was happening up to the end.

There was no pain, I didn't have cancer or other problems. My body was just plain worn out. I slept more and ate less, which were classic symptoms. My Dory had died two years earlier, and I missed her terribly.

As I lay dying, I didn't think I would be joining her in some afterlife. We both would be gone. That was fine. I didn't want to go on in this decrepit body without her at my side.

I wasn't Dylan. I wanted to go gently into that dark night.

That evening tunnel vision set in as I faded away. I don't know if there was a smile on my face, but there should have been.

Chapter 3

I awoke to voices. Was there an afterlife after all?
They weren't in English as I knew them, but they
had a familiar sound and cadence.

I lay there with my eyes closed, afraid to look at
what was happening. As the voices continued, I
began to make out words. It was as though a
foreign language was being translated as I listened.

Pretty soon, I was able to track the conversation.
These people seemed concerned for the life of their
young Baron who had been thrown from a horse.

He had hit his head and had a large bump form. It
didn't bleed, but they expected death from the
injury as they had seen similar ones many times.

I wondered why they didn't understand that it was
a hematoma and that death would ensue if the
swelling wasn't reduced.

A harsh voice said, "He needs liquid, or he will
surely die."

That made sense. The next thing I knew, a bitter
liquid was dripping on my lips. I involuntarily
licked what I identified as a bad, weak beer and
opened my eyes.

"He's awake!"

What is going on? Where is this young Baron?

Somehow I recognized the man as John Steward, the Steward of my castle.

How did I know this man and understand the language he was speaking? As I had these thoughts, he felt the back of my head.

"Abbot, the swelling has gone down. He will live," John said.

"Praise the lord the fount of all that is good."

I don't know who this guy is, but I better keep my nonreligious beliefs to myself.

To say I was confused would be putting it mildly. Why did these people think I was the Baron?

"My Lord, can you speak?"

I tried to speak up, but I could only mumble unintelligible words. As I tried to put my thoughts together, I heard another person in my head. They were raging about being shoved aside.

"At least he understands us. Let's hope the damage hasn't ruined his mind."

"Water," I managed to say.

John Steward raised my head and let me sip what I now identified as small beer. Wherever I was, the water was not considered drinkable. And that didn't bode well.

The small beer cleared my throat enough that I could talk.

"What happened?" I asked.

"That new war horse threw you, My Lord," John answered.

"How long ago?"

"Three days, we thought we had lost you."

"I need to relieve myself."

"You will be too weak to stand. Let me help you."

"I don't need help."

The steward didn't argue with me. He just caught me when I started to fall.

He laughed. "As stubborn as ever, I see."

"John, I knew you would catch me if I fell."

Abbot stepped into the conversation.

"What year is it, my Lord?"

"Do you want to know the year and wear my piss, or will you wait?"

"I think I will wait."

At that, John led me to a garderobe.

I whispered to him.

"What is the year?"

"The year of our Lord seven hundred and fifteen," he replied.

"Thanks."

"As I thought, your wits are not all there yet. The Abbot doesn't like you. He thinks you want to destroy his order."

"Why would I destroy them?"

"The church is claiming your best land. They claim your father left it to them to buy his way into heaven."

"Do they have it in writing?"

"No, they claim he did it in his last confession."

"Who took his confession."

"The Abbot with no one else to hear."

"I see."

I did see. Attempted theft, pure, plain, and simple. I had many things to learn about my situation, but here was something I could take care of at once.

My strength was coming back as John helped me. I wondered if he was real or a hallucination.

" John, was the horse that threw me examined?"

"Yes, a sharp stone was found under his saddle."

In 2010 it wouldn't be enough evidence for a prosecutor to take to a jury. Here I was Judge, Jury, and Executioner.

These thoughts weren't mine but of that unseen occupant in the back of my mind.

"I need the Abbot to show me the lands I'm giving up. Have him meet me on the top of the tower."

How I knew that we were on the top floor of the Keep, I didn't know. But I knew the steps along the far wall led to the top of the building.

I made my way up to the top as John went across the room to summon the Abbot to ascend the tower as I had summoned him. John waited below. It was heavy going, but I made it up the steps.

As I pictured, the top had a surrounding wall with crenelations to allow archers to fire. I looked over the edge and saw it was clear below.

When the Abbot cleared the steps, I grabbed him by the top of his hooded robe and shoved him off the tower. A sickening thud followed a brief yell.

"No one steals what is mine."

I was horrified by what I had done. Who or what am I?

My unseen companion radiated with satisfaction. He had his revenge and seemed to fade from my mind. His personality was gone, but his knowledge was still there.

I knew the names and jobs of the people I encountered but almost nothing about them. I would have to be careful about how I approached them.

What I had seen so far was familiar and, again, unfamiliar. It was as though I was in an alternate *Cornwall*. I doubted if I would ever understand what had happened. I couldn't go back. I had died.

My engineering common sense told me to make the best of this world. It is the only one that I have.

At least I wasn't a ninety-two-year-old man facing this strange situation. Without a mirror, it was hard to tell my physical shape.

Looking at my arms, legs, and chest, I was in good shape and probably in my mid-twenties. I didn't have any gross deformities, at least from how the

Steward and the Abbot looked at me before his demise.

A commotion came from down below, interrupting my thoughts.

The Abbot's body had been found.

My Steward came up to the top of the tower and asked me what had happened.

"The Abbot tried to prove that man can fly like a bird. He was wrong."

"It's a shame that he didn't try some time ago. He has been a pain for the last two years," John said.

"Who will replace him?"

"The Bishop in York appoints them, but it will take a while for word to reach him, a decision to be made, and the replacement to join the monastery. In the meantime, you can make a temporary replacement."

"Do you know a strong candidate locally?"

"Friar Luke, the Senior Monk, would be a good replacement. He is only interested in copying books and illustrating them. He doesn't seem interested in expanding the church's lands."

"Then I will appoint him. I wonder what it would take to make it permanent."

"The going rate for this Abbey has been two hundred silvers."

"Do we have enough in the treasury?"

"You must have taken a harder knock than we thought. We are rich right now. We have over twenty thousand silver on hand."

"Humor me, how did we obtain that?"

"You don't remember that Welsh merchant caravan we raided?"

I held my head and faked it.

"How could I forget! I must have really cracked my head. It is a wonder I am alive."

Oh, if he only knew the wonder of me being alive.

"Have the message about the Abbot's delusion of being able to fly sent accompanied by two hundred and fifty silver with our recommendation that Friar Luke be appointed Abbot."

"I will, My Lord, and there are a couple of other people I suggest be given flying lessons," he said.

"All in good time. If done too often, people might wonder."

"That's a shame."

"Others could try swimming with heavy clay boots."

"What an original idea!"

Thank you, Cosa Nostra. I also had to wonder where these thoughts were coming from. This ruthless streak wasn't part of Jim Fletcher. And it was frightening how calmly my Steward accepted it.

I would have to be careful if this was the norm of the day and age. Do unto others takes a whole new meaning.

Suddenly, I felt weak.

John Steward had to help me down the steps. Once back in bed, a simple pallet raised above the floor. I was given a bowl of stew.

It was good, which was a surprise. I had expected gruel or some tasteless dish. At least one fear was settled. I wouldn't starve to death.

Starving was far from my worst fear. I was afraid of the monster lurking inside me. Thankfully it seemed to leave me after I threw the Abbot off the tower.

It must have been thought that the Abbot was the one who tried to kill him. Once its revenge was accomplished, it moved on. Then why did I bring up concrete boots?

I realized this was a more dangerous age. There were no police. Maybe no laws, at least for the Nobles.

Was it the luck of the draw that I came back as a Noble? Maybe there is a larger plan in effect. If so, whose plan? Maybe I had better go to church.

After eating my stew, I asked John Steward to help me to my room. The pallet I had been laying on was in the main hall. Why there, I didn't know. There was a lot that I didn't know.

The Steward helped me down a hallway to my room. It wasn't far as this castle wasn't big as castles go. It was more like a fortified keep.

I asked why I had been on a pallet in the main hall.

"So, we could watch you. We knew someone was trying to kill you. It would be harder with you in the center of things. I had men detailed to watch any that approached you."

That made sense. I reminded myself that even though these people didn't have my scientific advantages, they weren't stupid. Thinking about it enough times, I might remember.

It was late in the afternoon, and I fell asleep immediately.

Chapter 4

Awake and alone for the first time, I tried to take stock of what I knew.

I had died, or at least I thought I did. No matter what, I wasn't in that body any longer.

The body I was in was younger, much younger, maybe around twenty-four. Not only younger but in excellent shape. It reminded me of when I was in World War II. Lean and mean.

I understood what was being said even though it appeared to be a different language. The language was one I had never heard spoken, and I had been to many different places in my previous life.

Yet the flow and accent seemed familiar. I had been somewhere where this language was spoken, but the words had changed, while the accent and cadence remained the same.

Then there was the stranger that had been inside my head. The stranger was now gone. They disappeared after taking control of my body to throw the Abbot off the tower.

The only thing that made sense was that the previous Baron knew the Abbot had tried to kill him. Actually, it looked like the Abbot had succeeded, and I had been inserted into the soon-to-be vacant body. That certainly spoke of god-like powers.

I wondered if that question would ever be answered.

There was also a leftover tendency for violence. Even though I had been through three wars, my reactions were harsher than normally warranted.

Was it the new me or a response to this day and age?

Thinking of this day and age made me wonder what the current date was and whether this was my old world or a different one.

Maybe it was some dying dream? Who knew, who cared? Dream or not, it was the hand that had been dealt, and I could play it or let events take over.

I suspect letting events take over wouldn't end well. I would play this hand.

So, I was here. This place reminded me of Cornwall for some reason. Dory and I had visited it several times. We loved the little fishing villages.

The only thing wrong with that thought was that I couldn't smell the ocean. What I did smell was too many humans in too small of a space with little knowledge of good sanitation practices.

I would have to change that. In the meantime, I had to learn more about my circumstances. How could I do this without raising John Steward's suspicion even more?

I thought for a few minutes and came up with a solution. I reflected on myself in the horrible-smelling garderobe. That was something else I had to change. That and inventing toilet paper.

Many things to do and so little time. Heaving a sigh I went looking for breakfast.

I found Steward in the main hall. He was having the same meal I had yesterday. While good, it could get boring. More change.

I didn't know what I called him most of the time. I weaseled and addressed him as, "My friend, I have some questions for you."

From his startled look, I had never called him a friend before. He didn't seem upset, just surprised.

"Who besides us knows about the merchant's silver?"

He got a pensive look.

"As you know, the merchants didn't have much silver, maybe five hundred as travel money. We got the silver when we sold the merchandise in Saltash."

This information gave me something to work with. In my time, Saltash was a small fishing port upstream from Plymouth.

"Then the merchants in Saltash knew I have gained much silver," I said.

"True, and that means the Baron of Saltash knows about it."

"When will he attack?"

"It is too late in the season, harvesting is about over, but snow will fly soon. The Baron will wait until spring to attack."

"Then we have that much time to get ready for him."

"My Lord, counting himself, he has six armored Knights. We have none."

"I have an answer for that."

"What?"

"Crossbows."

"Crossbows don't have enough power to penetrate armor and take too long to wind."

"I know how to make a stronger bow and wind it faster."

He didn't ask me to explain, but his face was easily read. He thought that I must have been brain-damaged by that fall.

"Tell me how many people I currently support in the castle," I said.

Now he knew for certain I had brain damage.

"Counting cooks, maids, armsmen, the blacksmith, stablemaster, brewer, bakers, and washerwomen about fifty."

"Take me on a tour of the castle."

"Very well, though we did the fall tour less than a month ago."

"Please humor a knocked in the head, addlepated Baron."

I was attempting to put him at ease by acknowledging my weakness, at least what he perceived as a weakness.

"Follow me."

"I notice the rushes on the floor look fresh."

"Yes, the quarterly replacement just occurred. That is one improvement that you have made that seems to work. Most rushes are only replaced once in the spring.

He continued, "That and banning pigs from the hall. We could train the dogs to go outside, but pigs went where they wanted."

"Maybe I'm not so addlepated."

He laughed. "That was before your fall."

Good, laughter is a sign that he isn't as worried as earlier. At least, I hope so.

We go to the kitchen. It was a small building separated from the main castle. I knew this was to prevent kitchen fires from spreading to the main building. This design would last for over a thousand years.

The danger was caused by cooking with wood which could be unpredictable when burning. Ovens moved up on my list of things to invent.

Before inventing a cook stove, I had to find out how much the local Blacksmith knew about metals and their compositions.

Steward called Cook over. Around thirty, hard to tell with their different lives, she was short and round, just as I imagined a castle cook would look. Her blond hair and strong arms were perfect for the part.

John asked the Cook how many scullery maids she now had.

"Five today, but Sally is about to have a babe, so I will lose her for a few weeks."

I broke in:

"Hire another from the village."

"That wouldn't be fair to the village girl. She would only work for a few weeks and then be let go," Cook said.

"You have my permission to keep her on full-time."

"We won't have enough work to keep the idle hands busy."

I left it as a cryptic:

"We will."

I didn't say that it would take another full-time person to keep this place clean. It is a wonder everyone wasn't dead from food poisoning.

Our next stop was the bakery. I was introduced to Robert Baker. Tall and thin, he didn't match my image of a baker. That was until I remembered that sugar is a rarity.

His area was neat and clean, opposite the kitchen. Note to self. Eat baked goods, not kitchen prepared. My modern stomach couldn't handle the kitchen foods.

Wait, I don't have a modern stomach anymore. This stomach had been living off the foods. Still, better to be careful.

Our next stop was the blacksmith shop. Predictably the Blacksmith was named Thomas Smith. He was a giant by local standards. Every bit of six foot two inches and two hundred and sixty pounds with almost no fat.

His soot and cinder-stained skin matched his dark brown hair. I doubted if it could ever be cleaned.

"What are you working on today, Master Smith?"

He grinned a huge, gapped tooth grin at the promotion. I didn't realize it at the time, but I had the privilege of declaring a trade level.

Oops.

"My Lord, the same as on most days, I'm repairing broken gear."

"What metals do you work with the most?" I asked.

"Tin, lead, copper, and iron when we get it."

"There's not much iron available. What ore is found is shipped to Saltash for selling."

"Ore or refined metal?"

"Ore, of course, My Lord, we have difficulty achieving the heat from our local woods. Even charcoaled wood doesn't work well."

"Have you tried coal?"

"You mean that black stone that burns."

"Yes, do you have any?"

"A few pieces."

"May I see it, please?"

The Blacksmith went to a back shed to collect a piece of coal. While he was gone, John Steward asked why I was saying "Please," to a commoner.

I smiled as I told John.

"He's a valued member of our community. He has earned the 'Please'."

John Steward shook his head. He didn't know what to make of the changes in his young Baron. They didn't seem bad, just different.

Smith returned with a chunk of black anthracite coal. It should burn clean and hot.

"This doesn't burn well?"

"No, look," he said tossing it on the bed of burning charcoal. The coal slowly started to burn.

"As you can see, it burns slowly and doesn't get hot."

It dawned on me what was different about this setup. There were no bellows. I leaned over the bed of coals and blew on the coal, which was starting to glow. When I blew on it, it flared up for a moment.

"Get with a leather worker and make a device to blow air."

"What would it look like," asked the puzzled Smith.

Using a piece of charcoal from his supply, I sketched out a hand-operated bellows.

"This device will provide more oxygen so the coal will burn hotter."

"What is oxygen?"

Thinking quickly, I stated, "Air."

If this was when I was beginning to think it was, the word oxygen hadn't been invented yet. One more thing to be careful about.

From Steward's frown, he was once again wondering about me.

The Smith asked, "This will create enough heat to melt iron ore?"

54

"Yes."

"If it does, we will become rich."

"Rich is good!" I spoke.

With that, we left for our next stop, the arrow shop. There I met, wait for it, Mark Fletcher. I wondered if he was a distant ancestor.

Fletcher was turning by hand a small lathe to create arrows.

"Where did you get this machine?" I asked surprised.

Fletcher was a small man and whipcord lean. I later learned he had been a Scout or Ranger before he took an arrow to his knee. What we had called a million-dollar wound in the twentieth century.

Here it might be worth less as he could have died from infection.

"It was made by my grandfather, who learned how from his grandfather. I was told that the ancient Romans invented it. It makes a better arrow than any done by hand," Fletcher said.

Having a lathe, even a small one, gave me an advantage for future developments.

"Could you make a large lathe to create arrows this big?" I used my hands to demonstrate an arrow about three inches in diameter and three feet long.

Fletcher grew excited, "My grandfather talked of machines that could fire an arrow like that. We could never figure out how to turn a lathe that big."

"Have you thought of a waterwheel?"

"No, My Lord, what is a waterwheel."

I had stepped into it again. From Steward's look, I had some fast talking to do.

"I will explain later."

"Yes, My Lord."

I noticed that people were glad to have a normal conversation with me, but as soon as I brought up a concept foreign to them, it was, "My Lord."

Our last stop was the Castle armory. The title was more impressive than the reality. It was a locked room that had racks of poorly made spears with bronze heads.

There were barrels of arrows, but not enough to fight a real battle, much less a war.

There were a dozen crossbows hanging from hooks. I could see why no one was impressed by them. They looked like kids' toys.

I had seen enough for today. My body was still recovering from the fall and being bedridden.

I also suspected I was in for an intense grilling by John Steward.

Chapter 5

I returned to my room at a glacial pace. I hoped that John Steward would take a hint that I was hurting and out of energy. No such luck. He accompanied me all the way.

"John, you don't have to follow me to my room. I can get there on my own."

"I'm worried about your safety, My Lord. I will be with you all the way."

What can you say to that?

When we got to my room, I staggered to my bed. I was hanging on by a thread.

Steward closed the door and started grilling me.

"Who are you? Are you a demon?"

I sighed. There was no getting out of this.

"No, I'm not a demon nor an angel."

"I know you aren't an angel. They would not have thrown the Abbot off the roof. They would have cast him straight to hell."

I thought to myself, 'tell us how you really feel about the Abbot.'

"I will tell you my story if you promise not to interrupt until I'm finished."

"All right."

"Over a thousand years from now, I will lay on my death bed at the age of ninety-two. I had a wonderful education in building things. It was a lifelong pursuit, but it was a waste of such a wonderful education.

"Instead of dying, I woke up in this body. I could use your language even though I didn't know what it was. It has gotten much better and now feel like I have used it all my life.

"My original language, American English, has many words that yours doesn't, so there are still some difficulties."

"Why do you have more words?" Stewart asked.

"Because many things change and advance in the next thousand years. We had to create new words for them.

"I see."

I wasn't about to explain airplanes, much less sending men to the moon.

"When I threw the Abbot from the tower, it was as though the other person in my body took control. Once that was done, I felt him leave."

"So, the previous Baron is gone?"

"Yes."

John Steward crossed himself saying, "Thank you, Lord."

I don't think he meant me.

He looked at me. "The man whose body you took was evil and would have destroyed us all. He cared nothing for anyone but himself. He knew we were short of food to make it through this winter and decided to let the peasants die off saying they could always breed more."

"But you have all that silver."

"He was going to buy knights and men-at-arms to conquer the surrounding Baronies.

"He was treacherous. The Welsh caravan was taken by poisoning the guard's food and then killing them in their sleep. It has stained my soul that I was part of such an action."

"John, we must talk much more about moving forward, but now I need rest."

"Rest well, Lord James."

"Wait, what did you call me?"

"By the name of your body, Lord James, Baron James Owen-nap."

The name was too much. I bid him goodnight and fell into bed.

*****

I lay in bed for a while in the morning, hoping it was all a dream. It wasn't. Why wasn't I dead and gone? It would be much easier.

Having the same name in both lives? The same name was God's territory. The problem is that I had never believed in the God of Christianity.

One thing for certain, God's plan or not, I was here and had to do the best I could. But I had absolutely no idea what that was.

On that cheerful note, I got up to start my day.

In my previous life, starting my day consisted of relieving myself, showering, brushing my teeth, and shaving.

Here I had to relieve myself in that terrible smelling garderobe. If nothing else, I would introduce a sanitation system.

Breakfast was being served in the main hall. It was porridge made from oatmeal. Milk and sugar would have made it more palatable. Even grinding the oats finer would have been an improvement. That and a mug of small beer set me up for the day.

Maybe a different diet would beat out sanitation as the first invention.

John Steward joined me as I finished up.

"Baron James, would you like to see the village?"

"I didn't know we had a village."

"It isn't much, but it is ours."

As we spoke, an old woman took my bowl. She wiped it clean with a dirty rag and used it for another man's meal.

Yep, sanitation just moved back to the top of the list.

Outside of the main gate of the Keep was a group of hovels, giving a new meaning to the word squalor.

They were made from wood and clay with thatched roofs. Not a single one had any windows. My list of things to do kept getting longer.

What passed as the main street was a muddy mess. It suited the hogs laying on the road. Several small boys were having a mud fight. They were the most cheerful sight I had seen since waking.

"John Steward, you didn't seem upset about the Abbot's death. Why?"

"He was as evil as the former Baron."

"He wanted the power here by claiming the land for the church so it wouldn't owe taxes and the Baron wouldn't be able to support his Barony. But the Baron inadvertently thwarted his plan by raiding the merchant caravan. That is why the Abbot attempted to murder the Baron."

"Nice people."

"God decided to send you here to save us all."

That stopped me cold. The foundation of my disbelief was shaking. However, this was something that had to be taken on faith, and I had none.

"That may be. What matters is that I'm here and have to make a life. I refuse to live in this squalor, so I will change things."

"What changes?" He looked hopeful.

"You talked earlier about not having enough food for the winter. What is the situation?" I asked.

"As it stands, I guess we will lose half our population if you sell the crops."

"We can't allow that. We will have to keep the food."

"You can't do that. It would be best if you had the silver to hire more men-at-arms to defend your Barony.

"There is no doubt that Baron Saltash will attack in the spring," Steward finished.

"My wealth is not my silver; it is my people. People can earn silver. Silver is a tool that has a fixed value. People make things grow in worth."

"That is a strange way to look at it."

"Look at it this way. If you bury ten silvers in the spring and dig it up in the fall, you have ten silvers. What will it be worth in the fall if you bought ten silvers worth of seed and planted it in the spring?"

"What if the crop fails?"

"That is part of the risk, reward cycle. The greater the risk, the greater the reward," I said.

"These are strange thoughts. I must think about them."

"In the meantime, where do we store grain."

I was led to a rectangular building on a raised platform that had a slight slope for drainage. With slots near the roof to allow ventilation.

One end was near a ramp. The ramp ended about five feet from the door of the building. Boards would be extended to enter the building. The platform and ramp prevented rodents from getting to the grain.

This building was amazing, as the earliest records of this design were made around the thirteenth century in my world.

"Who designed this type of storage?" I asked.

"I don't know. It has always been here."

"It is a good design. Better than the beehive design."

"Beehive, what is a beehive?"

"Don't we have a beekeeper?"

A short "No," ended that conversation.

"Where can we buy enough grain to fill this large granary? It doesn't look like our crops would fill it."

"Soon, caravans will take grain to the market in Saltash. We can buy it from them. It is from the

Barons further north. It will be shipped to Londonium and sold."

"Would the caravans sell it to us at market price?"

"They would be glad to. It would save them several day's journeys."

"Is there much grain taken to Saltash from other areas?"

"Not to my knowledge. It all comes past us," Steward said.

"So, if we bought all the grain, then we could sell what we didn't need to the merchants in Saltash."

"Yes, we could."

"If we own all the grain, we could set the price."

John smiled. "We could charge enough to pay for the grain we keep."

"We might even make a few more silver on top of that."

"This is going to be interesting," John said.

"Not just interesting. Our people will live through the winter, and we will still have the silver."

"You will be able to hire all the men-at-arms you need."

"We won't have to hire any," I said.

"How can that be?"

"I haven't told you I was a soldier in my country's army. I was a general officer in command of over thirty thousand men. I have fought in three different wars. I think I can build a small army to defeat the Baron.

"Now we need this granary cleaned out. After cleaning, all openings are to be sealed, and smoky firepots burnt to kill off any insects."

"I will make it happen. Men in the village perform labor as part of their taxes."

"Also, send runners to the nearest Barons offering to buy their grain at the market price when they bring it here," I said. "Another question, how many roads or trails are used to come through my Barony?"

"There are three roads that enter Gwen nap. They join and run past our castle."

"So, we will know of all grain going to market."

"Yes, My Lord."

I noticed that whenever I impressed Steward, I became 'My Lord.'

I also learned that my Barony was Gwen nap. The names Saltash and Gwen nap were familiar, but I didn't think they were adjacent in my world.

I was beginning to accept this was a different world than the one I was born into. I hoped it was true so I wouldn't set up a time-travel paradox.

We traipsed through the mud around the rest of the village. There was a small village bakery, an apothecary, a wheelwright, and a tannery on the edge of town.

It was nearly noon, and I was hungry. When I mentioned this to John, he was surprised. It seems like we only get two meals a day. No wonder people at breakfast ate so much.

On the way back to the Keep, I asked John, "How much labor do we have above the normal workload of the Keep and the Village?"

I had to explain what I meant by that. It seems that this century didn't have words like workload.

"Ten men and a few boys don't have a regular occupation. They have trouble feeding their families and cause the most problems."

"What sort of problems?"

"Petty theft and drunkenness."

"After lunch, have them brought to the Keep. I need to offer them a job. Also, how much would they need to have a reasonable standard of living."

Once more, a term had to be explained. Standard of living wasn't a concept here and now. Since standard and living were both words in this Cornish dialect, they came across as the words in use.

When I brought up a concept that Cornish had no word for, the English word came into play. We would end up with a language like Spanglish.

After eating the last of the morning's oatmeal, I met with the unemployed of the village. I told the men and boys they were now on the village payroll. I would pay them a penny a day for five days of work each week.

They would be performing whatever tasks they were assigned. All jobs would be to improve the life of the village.

As expected, most of them were happy. Two drunkards, by their looks, asked what would happen if they didn't want the job.

"Feel free to move on," I said.

"What if we don't want to work or move on?"

"John Steward, seize these men and give them ten strokes with a cane for being stupid."

"Yes, My Lord!"

I asked the others, "Are there any more questions?"

They were silent as they watched the two hauled away. This situation made me think of the Jamestown colony. No work, no food.

Chapter 6

On our walk around the village, John pointed out the village midden. This gulley that ran behind a row of houses was where they threw their trash away.

Archeologists would be thrilled to find this in the future. It gave a glimpse into the life of the village.

Not everyone used the midden, though. Some villagers threw junk out into their yards. I had John Steward assign our new village workforce to clean up all the trash in the area.

In the future, the midden would have to be further away from the living quarters, but I wanted to start changing how people looked at the village. There would also be fines for those who trashed the place.

There was one large stream that provided the drinking water for the village. As you might guess, livestock were in the stream above where water was drawn. This practice had to change.

Also, the disposal of human waste was questionable. John and I took a walk down the stream. We identified a spot that was close to the path along the stream. The water was shallow, and the bottom was sandy. Waste could be dumped here and broken up by washing across the sand, and the current would take it away.

Not as good as a septic tank, but better than a cesspool. The best part was it could be put to use immediately.

I direct John to set up a daily collection of the nightsoil. Our village task force would perform this chore.

John asked how the nightsoil would be transported to the stream. We went back to the Blacksmith. He had plenty of copper since it was mined locally. I would provide a cart from the castle.

Keep, fortress, castle, what should it be called? Everyone varied it in their conversation, sometimes even in the same sentence. It was driving me bats. Maybe I'm a little OCD about it.

The blacksmith was to make an open container about the size of half a fifty-five-gallon drum. One end would have a removable section. Waste would be dumped into the container. When full, the cart would be taken to the stream, and the waste dumped.

There would be a second container filled with fresh water. This water would be used to rinse the chamber pots. Water would be scooped into the pots, swirled around, and dumped into the nightsoil bin.

Not perfect, and there would be spillage, but it would be an enormous improvement over the current state of affairs.

I left it to John to negotiate the price with the Blacksmith. I'm glad I did. I would have paid ten times too much.

I had been thinking about the animals in the stream. Animal waste would be a problem because it could be in the stream out of sight of the village.

The only quick solution I could think of was fencing along the river for at least a mile upstream. It would be the zig-zag style or a worm fence with each run at a 60-degree angle.

The good thing about a zigzag was that you didn't need to dig post holes. The corner post of the fence could be set upon a flat rock.

A man skilled in using an ax and a wedge could cut 150-200 10-foot rails in one day, and a man adept at erecting fences could lay 200 yards per day.

The land on both sides of the river would need to be surveyed, and a shallow crossing found to run the fence across. The fence wouldn't last, but it would keep animals out of the river and provide a clean water source.

A well would be better. That digging a well was not as simple as one might think. A lot had to be taken into consideration. Digging a well is where my funky memory came into play.

In the long run, a clean, fenced-off, spring-fed lake with an aqueduct to the village would be best. The Romans had developed these into a science. I knew how, but we didn't begin to have the manpower to build one.

I asked John Steward if anyone in the area had put in a permanent well before. He didn't know of anyone but would ask around.

We continued our village tour, with me being introduced to the villagers along the way. Of course, I forgot the first names immediately. I did remember that we had a good selection of trades.

I met a Miller, Stonemason, Carpenter, Weaver, Shoemaker, Thatcher, Bowyer, Wheelwright, Butcher, Merchant (Grocer), and several Farmers.

These were all the last names and professions of those I met. As I said, first names escaped me.

Three names stuck out.

Our Potter, Olaf Erickson. One look confirmed the name. If I weren't assured that his grandfather was born in the village, I would have bet he just got off a dragon boat.

Tall and blonde, he was the picture of what a Viking looked like, at least in the movies I had seen.

The Candlemaker had no other name. Steward told me he had drifted into the village about ten years ago and set up shop. He had never given a name, so the villagers only referred to him as the Candlemaker, shortened to Candlemaker.

I suspected that there was a reason that he had never provided his true name. John assured me that while everyone thought the same, Candlemaker had never caused any problems.

With no problems in ten years, I decided to let it go. At least I would remember Candlemaker's name.

Then there was the Cabinet Maker, Mark Woodson. His father must have been a woodworker of some sort. We didn't converse long enough for me to find out.

While we had the basic trades covered, we were short a number of people I thought the village needed for a self-sustaining economy. We had the workers, but we didn't have the customers.

We either needed more people or to set up foreign trade. In this case, foreign trade would be with surrounding Baronies.

I had so many thoughts buzzing around that it was hard to keep track of them.

John and I returned to the Keep discussing some matters. I had to share my thoughts and get them moving, or I would forget them.

I explained to John that clean water was a must for the village. He had understood collecting the nightsoil and depositing it downstream. Everyone knew better than drinking water with a turd floating in it. So fencing the upstream portion of the river made sense.

He had a harder time understanding that small animals in the water could make you sick. I gave up trying to explain bacteria to him. It was good enough that he knew not to drink water with poop floating in it.

I would have to invent the microscope to prove my point. That, in turn, would mean glass making and grinding. We had a long way to go.

Since the nightsoil pick-up would start when the Blacksmith finished his part, it would probably be another ten days before that operation started.

In the meantime, my new village workers would build the fencing along the river. Based on what I knew about building zig-zag fences, it would take a crew of ten men about two weeks to accomplish the task. Assuming there were no obstacles along the river.

John and I headed to the tavern to discuss the fencing. He ordered two small beers to our table.

This stuff was not what I would call beer. It was almost like porridge you could drink. It had wheat floating in it, giving a new name to wheat beer.

At less than one percent alcohol, you would have to drink fast to get drunk. With it being so solid, I doubted if it could be done. With its strong wheat flavor, it wasn't that pleasant to drink.

It would take me a while to get used to it. Better yet, I would teach the Brewer how to make real beer after I got us a source of clean water.

Since it was a rare, nice day for fall in Cornwall, we decided to walk up the river to find out how difficult fencing the area would be.

There was only one area that would be difficult to fence, a large rocky protrusion next to the river. We discussed how to fence it when John realized that no cattle or sheep could get up there.

We laughed; no fencing would be needed. This protrusion would save us a hundred yards of fencing on this side of the river. And I was reminded that these people were as intelligent as I was.

We had to trek almost a mile and a quarter upstream before finding a spot to build a fence across the river. This barrier would stop livestock from walking down the river and pooping.

We would lose the fence across the river during high water events but replacing it would be easy.

We crossed the river to ensure that there were no surprises. I liked the fact that the locals were calling it a river. It was a stream at best. At fifty feet across and a depth of three feet, it was more like what we called creeks in Ohio. Well, most of us, the kids from West Virginia, called them cricks.

Nothing on the other side would prevent us from building a fence along the river's length. I had even thought about diverting water from the river to build a moat around my fortress.

The slow, shallow flow convinced me that any decent field engineer could drain my moat in no time, so that wasn't going to happen. What was going to happen was tall, thick concrete walls.

As soon as I invented concrete, that is. Mortar for bonding bricks and stone has been around for a long time, but we need cement and concrete.

The raw materials were all available locally. What we lacked was manpower.

I shared my concerns with John as we walked along the creek, crick, river. Whatever. He brought up a possible way of adding to our population.

The grain that would be soon passing by us was almost all the grain from the various Baronies. It was a long-standing practice in the area to let the people who grew the grain starve in the winter if they couldn't hide enough from the tax collectors.

Selling all the grain added to the Baron's ability to have a larger army. In turn, a larger armed force allowed him to send armed men with grain caravans to 'protect' them. The reason was to prevent the caravanner from absconding with the grain to feed their families.

The logic of all this escaped me. John suggested we let it be known that families who wanted to move to our Barony would be fed through the winter and given paid jobs.

This action would strengthen my Barony while weakening the others. What was there not to like? All we would have to do was ensure we had enough shelter for the new people. The grain we would buy would be more than enough to feed them.

When the grain caravans come, John will negotiate the grain purchase from the armed guards while several villagers mingle with the caravan workers explaining how they could avoid starvation for their families.

Stealing people from the Barons, even though they were going to allow them to starve, would eventually lead to war. But that seemed inevitable.

My next step would be to get together with the Blacksmith and Bowyer to start making crossbows which would take down Knights and their horses.

I had until the spring to get that done and train my men-at-arms in their use.

Chapter 7

I heard about a small church not associated with the Monastery or visible from the Keep.

"John, what can you tell me about the little church outside of town?"

"There isn't much to tell. There is a single priest in residence. He attends to the needs of the village and the Keep."

"How is he supported? I don't see that there is much money in circulation here." I asked.

"Mostly in kind, the locals give what food they can. He gives most of it to those who can't support themselves."

"Is there enough to keep the poor from starving?"

"Just barely," John said.

"Did the Baron contribute?"

"No."

"Let's take a walk over there. I want to meet the Priest."

As we walked John filled me in on the local Parish.

"It's poor. The Bishop in Saltash won't contribute to its upkeep. It is a wonder that Father Timothy hasn't starved."

"That will have to change. How much should a Priest receive to be the Keep's Chaplain?" I asked.

"Five silvers a week would be plenty. That is if Father Timothy didn't use it all to buy food for his poor."

"His poor? I thought they all belonged to me?"

"In the past, you wouldn't feed them as they contributed nothing to your Barony. Useless mouths, you called them."

What a bastard I had been. Yet I shouldn't throw too many stones until I learned what it took to survive in this day and age.

The little church wasn't anything fancy. Not the elegant Norman churches one thinks of from the Middle Ages. This building was a stone and wattle construction with a thatched roof. It could hold fifty people at the most.

As we approached, a tall thin man in dark robes in his early twenties came out of the church to greet us.
"Welcome. How may I help you today?"

"Father Timothy, I find myself in need of a Chaplain for the Keep. Would you accept that position for five silvers a week?"

To say that he was surprised was putting it mildly!

"Yes, yes, yes! I would be glad to accept the position."

The smile that lit up the dark-haired young man's face was a joy to see. It would win the heart of many a village maiden. I wondered if priests were allowed to marry at this time. A question for later.

"Also, for your information, no one in the village will starve this year. I'm buying all the grain that normally passes through to Saltash. It will feed all in the area, even those I called 'useless mouths.' After careful thought, I realize they could be useful in a way that profits all."

He looked fearful as he asked, "How can they be useful?"

"There will be many new jobs in the village for which they can be hired, even the blind and the lame. Even the simple will have a task they can perform."

"How will you pay for all of that?"

"Do not speak to others of this, but the price of grain in Saltash is about to go up."

The sudden look of comprehension spoke well of his intelligence.

"You mean the bishop will have to pay more for his daily bread?"

"Yes."

"How wonderful and elegant of a solution to our problems!" He exclaimed.

"Father, on another note, what does the Bible say about cleanliness?"

I knew full well that the saying, 'Cleanliness is next to Godliness,' is attributed to John Wesley far in the future. However, Wesley based it upon many biblical references to cleanliness.

"I will have to reread portions of Leviticus and Genesis, but I think God desires cleanliness."

"So do I, and for a good reason. I recently learned of an old text which described small animals, so small they couldn't be seen. They live in nightsoil and can make one ill."

"I would love to see this text."

"Alas, the man who owned it has moved on."

I went on to explain about collecting the village nightsoil and dumping it downstream so that it wouldn't contaminate the village and fencing in the

84

stream above where the village drew its water. I didn't go into a well or aqueduct at this time. I didn't want to overload the man's thinking' or end up being burned for a witch!

When I told him about this, he got a thoughtful look.

"What about the people who live downstream from the village?"

At that, I let out a nasty oath.

"I didn't think of that. Downstream changes things.

"John, we must find a natural depression and line it with clay. Each day the new contents will be covered with quicklime."

"What is quicklime?"

"Burnt limestone. It will cause the nightsoil to dry out and lessen the foul odor."

It then could be used as fertilizer, but I had western civilization's aversion to doing that.

I no sooner thought that than Father Timothy spoke up.

"We use animal waste on fields to improve crops. Why can't we use human waste if it is dried into dust."

"Some people find it disturbing, but there is no real reason we can't," I said.

"Especially if all the waste from animals from the village is included."

I hadn't even thought of that. Hogs were living in the streets. We needed to change that immediately.

I like this guy. He is sharp.

I thought about bringing up midwives and cleanliness but decided to wait a few days.

"John, see to getting Father Timothy his first week's payments in advance. Consider it a hiring bonus."

From their strange looks, I had just introduced a new concept to this day and age.

"I will see to Father Timothy getting his 'hiring bonus' immediately."

It was as though he was tasting a new set of words to see how they felt.

Leaving an ecstatic Father Timothy with instructions to join us at the Keep for supper and to receive his payment, we went to the Monastery.

The Monastery was currently without an Abbot as I had tipped him over the top of the Keep's tower. They greeted us with smiles. Leaving no one to think he wasn't missed and that they were silently rejoicing in his demise. It seemed as if no one thought the Abbot had taken up flying, at least of his own volition.

The senior Monk, Friar Luke, welcomed us to the Monastery. At this time, monasteries had specialties. This Monastery copied manuscripts. Almost all Monasteries practiced copying, but not to this degree.

They also didn't spend as much time on illustrations as others. The senior Monk was almost apologetic when he explained that his group saw the need to get more knowledge out into the world rather than pretty pictures. His words, not mine.

"Do you only do religious works, or are you amenable to others, such as a text on how to build something?" I asked.

He looked hesitant to answer. After thinking for a moment, he replied.

"There is no theological reason we couldn't do it. The question is could we sell the text? There is a ready market for religious text, but I have never heard of what you are requesting."

"I would pay you upfront for copying documents."

"Then we would be pleased to do as many as you want, as long as the price is reasonable."

I liked this business guy. I came prepared with a test to see how he thought.

"Could I have some ink and a piece of parchment? Used will do."

He sent a junior Monk to collect the paper and ink. Once I had the materials, I brought out one silver coin. I selected it for the sharpness of its impressions. It hadn't seen much circulation.

I poured several drops of ink on the head's side of the coin. I don't know who was represented by this coin, and it didn't matter.

I pressed the inky surface of the coin onto the paper. I repeated this five times.

The first time there was too much ink, and it smeared. The second impression was a clear one of the head. The third and fourth were identical to the second. The fifth was much fainter as the ink was used.

"Now imagine if it was a letter on the coin instead of a head. Now make the coin narrower and use all the letters of the alphabet, and you can spell out a word. You could make several impressions from one inking and reink as often as needed. Think about this and what it would do to your productivity."

To say that he looked like a fish as his eyes got big and mouth hung open would be putting it mildly.

"Think about this, then talk to the Blacksmith about making the letters. They call the metal letters type, where I learned this."

I handed him the coin as John and I turned to leave. I'm certain he will demonstrate this to the other Monks as soon as we leave.

John told me he had doubts about my origin, but now he had none. My change in attitude was beyond the ex-Baron. The knowledge I had just shared was mind-boggling in its implications. There was no way the ex-Baron could have thought of that.

My first thought is, what do you call a person whose body you have taken over? The possessed? No way, that spoke of the devil. I suppose ex-Baron worked as well as anything. We couldn't use it around others.

We stopped at the Blacksmith on our short journey to the Keep. He had something he wanted to show me.

It was a crude hand-operated bellows. The smith excitedly let me know that he had been able to get coal hot enough to weld iron. That meant it was almost two thousand degrees. Well over the eight hundred degrees normal burning achieved.

This temperature was much hotter than he could get with wood. He wanted to switch to coal for all of his work. All that was needed was better bellows and a reliable source of coal.

Even though we didn't mine coal in the Barony, John assured us several coal seams were near the surface locally.

The Blacksmith had talked to the Tanner and the Cabinet Maker. They could make his bellows and had even come up with a design that was foot powered!

Encouraged by this progress, John and I went to dinner. At least I was encouraged. I think John was in a mild state of shock at how fast things were happening.

Word spreads fast in a small Village and Keep like ours. The fencing along the river and the daily pickup of nightsoil were the main topics of conversation. Father Timothy's being hired as the Keep Chaplain was God's blessing. I was now viewed as an open question.

Either I was God-touched or had a nefarious plan. The ex-Baron's reputation must have been bad because most wondered what my plan was.

No one told me this to my face. John later shared this over a glass of wine in my quarters. The wine was more like vinegar. Another item on my growing list of things to invent or improve.

I hoped Friar Luke would take the printing idea and run with it. He could have the credit for inventing the printing press. I needed to delegate as much as possible if I was going to accomplish anything.

Father Timothy told me most villagers liked keeping animals and nightsoil out of the water. Some didn't like change, but he assured me they would come around when threatened with damnation.

Threatening with damnation was a good reminder that I wasn't in Kansas anymore. On second thought, I don't think I had ever visited Kansas.

I doubted that I would ever have the chance now. The California gold fields were going to be a different story.

Chapter 8

The next morning, I asked John to accompany me to my office after the communal breakfast. The food was the same as yesterdays. This diet would get old fast.

I had to introduce new foods, or I would starve from boredom. Studies in the twentieth century proved that if someone were fed the same food over and over, they would lose weight. I believed it.

I would have to have a session with the cook but was afraid of what I would find in the kitchen. I put that off for a later time. I had more pressing questions for John.

"John, I need to talk to you in private. Let's go to my office after we are finished eating."

"Very well, My Lord."

I think he was teasing me now. At least, I hope so.

As we settled onto our stools, I made a mental note to have chairs with backs made. So much to do, so little time.

"John, what do we have in money, men, and natural resources?"

"The treasury has twenty-three thousand silvers, twenty of which came from that Welsh caravan. As far as men, we have twenty armsmen."

"How many able-bodied men are in the Barony?"

"I have no idea, maybe another one hundred. That excludes the hungry mouths," he said.

"How many of the one hundred are on farms?"

"All except those you hired to be village workers."

"So about ninety men. Are they all needed on the farms?" I asked.

"I think so."

"What about women that are surplus to farming requirements?'

"I have no idea. I would think none, as the excess women are destined to be farmers' wives or care for their parents in their old age."

"So, we don't know how many people may be available for other tasks." I paused to think.

"John, have you heard of the term 'census'?"

"No."

"It is an official count of all those present in the Barony. It would list each residence's occupants, names, sex, and age. We would track down all the homeless and list them the same way.

"Each residence, farm, or town would have its basic information written down. Such as how many cows, pigs, and other animals are on a farm. The number of acres being cultivated and how many were lying fallow."

"Why would you need that?" He asked.

"I'm going to introduce changes that will require more people. We need to employ those we have efficiently as possible."

"It also gives an idea how much in taxes might be owed."

His eyes lit up at that. Any Steward worth his salt wanted more taxes.

I asked John, "Who could we get to do this census? The census takers would have to be able to read and write. Plus, someone who the people would respond to."

He replied, "I wonder if some of the monks could be sent out, accompanied by some men-at-arms."

"That would work if the new Abbot would agree."

"Oh, I think he will. He isn't officially the Abbot yet."

94

"Good point. How many outlying farms do you think we have?"

"Probably seventy or so, I'm not certain," he said.

"We will also require the Monks to make a rough map of the areas they count."

The Steward thought for a moment and then spoke slowly.

"We will know more about your Barony than anyone has before."

Wait until he learns what surveying consists of.

"One of our first stops today will be to talk to the Abbot. I want to get this started as soon as possible."

"All right, My Lord."

I think the man is serious!

"I need to know what natural resources we know of."

"What do you mean by that?"

"What known coal seams are there. Any copper and tin deposits? Forests with hardwoods? Natural springs? Items found naturally in nature will have value to us."

He replied, "Again, there has never been a systematic search for them. Each farmer may know what is in their area, but no one tracks all of it."

"So, a census question will be what natural features are in the area. If someone has found a silver deposit, they may not want to share that information."

"I think we would know of that. No one has shown that kind of money around here."

"John, if it were my farm, I would keep the silver a secret. I would build a small furnace to melt the ore. Then I would take it to Saltash and leave it with a money lender. I might invest in some shipping ventures.

"I wouldn't spend like crazy where my neighbors could see. I would keep a good supply of food on hand. The family would live comfortably but not look rich."

John indignantly replied, "If we find someone like that, they will be hanged for the thieves they are."

"No, they won't be hanged. They will be given a portion of all the silver mined on their land. We will increase the size of the mine. They will get a small percentage of the output, but the output will be much larger than they could dig out by themselves."

"But you own all the land. They are renting from you," he said.

"That is another change in the future. I will sell the farmers the land."

"Why?"

"People who work on their own land to support their families work harder and make more for themselves. The more they make, the more they pay in taxes. The taxes will exceed the previous rents."

We then set out for the monastery to discuss using Monks for recording the census. We walked down the main road. I swore it smelled better already, and the collections hadn't even started yet.

One old lady stepped in front of us in the middle of the road.

"May I speak, Lord?"

"Yes, you may."

"People were grumbling about the new method of disposing of nightsoil. Father Timothy talked to them and explained that cleanliness is next to godliness. Do you agree with that?"

"I do. That is why the nightsoil is being taken away rather than tossed into the drinking water from the river. Before, we were drinking water with turds floating in it. I don't like that idea."

"But the water dissolved the dung, and it was gone."

"You are correct. It dissolved in the water, but it was not gone. When you steep tea, the solids dissolve and can't be seen. That doesn't mean they are gone."

She looked thoughtful.

"Then we have been drinking poop tea?"

"Yes, nasty thought, isn't it."

She smirked. "Oh, I can't wait to tell my neighbor she has been drinking poop. She has been the loudest complainer about setting her chamber pot outside."

"Tell her if she doesn't do that like everyone else, she will be known as a poopy breath."

The old lady was giggling as she walked on her way.

I turned to John, "That will do more to get people doing as we want than all the laws we could pass."

"I agree, My Lord."

I don't think I will ever get him to call me James.

At the Monastery, the Senior Monk, soon-to-be Abbot, greeted us profusely.

"What can I do for you today, My Lord?"

I explained a census to him and that we needed people who could read and write. As I spoke, I could see the wheels turning in his head. He was paying close attention and thinking about something.

"Of course, I expect to pay a silver a day per monk to your coffers. Also, I would pay to have two copies of the final census bound. One for here and one for the Keep."

You didn't have to be a mind reader to know his thoughts. At least about the money, the binding of the books was gravy. Not the money, but to be a custodian of such a document.

My only concern was that the books should be considered military secrets. I would have to impress that upon the Senior Monk later.

We discussed the logistics and timing of the census. John had a good suggestion. Have it announced in church for the village people and send runners to as many farms as possible.

We agreed that any silver mining wouldn't be discussed at this time. I had no evidence of any silver deposits on my land, but I had a gut feeling and wanted to approach the issue carefully.

Since I wanted this to happen as soon as possible, I asked for two monks to be identified as possible census takers. While the Abbot was fetching them, I wondered if I should bring up ASAP to them.

That would probably be going too far.

Two monks were brought to the Abbot's office. From the slovenly look of one of them, I wanted no part of him. I found people who took so little care of their appearance to be the same in their work.

Being the Baron has some advantages.

"That one will not do. Bring another Monk cleaner in their appearance."

The Senior Monk looked like he would challenge me but didn't. Instead, he signaled the dirty looking one to follow him.

While he was selecting another Monk, I took the opportunity to talk to the remaining Monk. His name was Brother Simon.

I explained what the job would be.

"I would love to help with the census. It would get me out of here and the endless copying."

I liked the good-looking young man's attitude. I also made a mental note to tell the accompanying men-at-arms to keep an eye on him and any young ladies he met.

He gave me a sample of his handwriting, which was more than sufficient for the project.

Another Monk was brought in, Brother Paul. He was swarthy looking and reminded me of a pirate. He also proved to be well-spoken and intelligent. There had to be a story behind him.

All the guards would have to watch the young Monks and the farm girls. But who would be watching the guards?

The two Monks, the Senior Monk, John, and I spent some time deciding upon the questions to be asked and a form to record them.

There would be one form for each residence or individual interviewed. They would be collated after they visited.

I thought I would have to explain collation to the Monks, but they understood what I meant.

While we were designing the forms, I numbered each item. That opened a can of worms earlier than I had planned.

What I thought would be an hour at the most turned into an all-day session as I explained Arabic numerals.

Once the concept of zero as a placeholder was understood, there was no stopping them. The two young Monks were fascinated with how quickly numbers could be added or subtracted.

The Senior Monk followed, but it was like demonstrating an adding machine on his subordinate's desk to him. He was interested but didn't envision himself using it.

When I demonstrated multiplication and division, it was like Saint Michael had descended to earth and taught lessons about how things worked.

That even got the Senior Monk's attention. John just sat there and took it all in.

We had worked through lunch, so I was ready to leave by dinner time. I left the Monks with a poorly written copy of the multiplication tables up through nine times nine.

I was asked if this was as high as you could multiply numbers. I quickly demonstrated four digits times four digits and told them this would have to wait for another time.

On the way back to the Keep, I expressed my concerns to John about the Monks and young farm girls and who would watch the men-at-arms.

He roared with laughter.

"The idea of a census told me you weren't telling a story about being someone else. The Arabic numbers confirmed that. Your lack of understanding of how things work here is absolute confirmation."

"What do you mean?"

"Any farm girl with child by someone who could read and write would be considered a rare prize on the marriage market."

He was right. I didn't understand. At least I had given the Steward a good laugh.

Chapter 9

It was becoming routine for John Steward and me to retire to my office after breakfast. There we would plan our day.

"John, what is our current food status for the winter if we don't send any grain to Saltash?"

"There will be empty bellies, but all strong enough would live through the winter."

"So, if we buy the grain shipments coming through and save some for ourselves, we will do quite well?"

"Better than the oldest grandfather can remember. You will be a hero to your people," he said.

"This morning let's check how the river fencing is coming along. Before that, though, there are several items that I need to start or follow up on."

"Such as?"

"The first thing on my list is to have my stinking garderobe cleaned! After that, it is to be cleaned every week," I said.

"Very well, My Lord, it will be done. It will be scheduled regularly. Maybe we could use it as a punishment detail."

"Especially the first time! Have them place fresh moss there every week. Also, the vinegar for the sticks needs to be replaced at that time. Come to think of it, fresh sticks to wrap the moss around every week. Also, have the nightsoil crew remove the dung pile that has accumulated below the garderobe. "

"Now, that will be a punishment." He laughed.

"From now on, the collection from that area is part of the daily routine. I have not looked at the Keep's latrines, but I suspect they are in the same condition. Have them cleaned and refreshed the same way. Once we have quicklime, we will use it whenever someone moves their bowels."

"Yes, My Lord."

"For goodness's sake, John quit with the 'Yes, My Lord.' Just say okay."

"What is, okay?"

"Okay, is a word from my time which means you will do as I asked or understand what I'm telling you, or if something is correct and works, you say it is okay."

"With that many meanings, how do you know what is meant?"

Maybe we aren't ready for okay.

"You win. Yes, My Lord works."

He grinned. "Yes, My Lord."

Now I know he is yanking my chain.

"Before I forget, are Priests allowed to marry?"

"That is a strange question. Priests have always been allowed to marry. Why do you ask?"

"That will change in the future. I think our Father Timothy will become a prime candidate once his change in fortune is known."

John chuckled as he replied, "He will be sought after by dark today. Word spreads fast."

"Another question, I didn't see any living quarters near the church."

"He sleeps in the church."

"That will have to change once a village girl catches him, but we will worry about that later."

"Yes, My Lo… uh, okay."

"Well done, John!"

My first attempt to destroy old English. Spanish and English melded in Spanglish. Old English and American English is Amlish? It doesn't matter; I'm the only one who will ever know.

106

We stopped at the cabinet makers to check on the fencing. And I wanted to order some chairs.

I had to make a rough sketch on a wax board that the cabinet maker kept for such occasions. I ended up ordering eleven chairs. Three for my office and eight for my Keep's main hall table. They were what I thought of as Captain's chairs. They had slightly curved backs, armrests, cushioned backs, and seats.

John Steward negotiated the price. Once more, I would have paid way too much. This bargaining was one of those moments I missed my Dory. She was excellent at it and enjoyed it.

Once in Singapore, she bargained an old merchant down so much that he had his wife take over. That was a sign of true respect for her skills. Those two women went at it for half an hour before completing the five Singapore dollars purchase. You could tell both women were happy. The price had nothing to do with it. It was the joy of the hunt, female style.

Later I asked Dory how much she had saved on the little vase.

She proudly told me, "Ten cents, American."

I was smart enough to keep my mouth shut.

Next, we stopped at the church and spoke to Father Timothy.

"Father, I want you to make several announcements at your Masses this week."

"What are they?"

"The first one is that a Monk accompanied by men-at-arms will visit every house in the Village. They will be taking what is called a census. The Monk will record the number of inhabitants, their sex, ages, and their primary occupation. Housewife is an occupation. If a person has a useful secondary skill that also needs to be reported."

"Why do you need to know all of that?" He asked.

"It is hard to plan if you don't know what to work with. We will send teams to the countryside to let them know they will also have a census taken."

"I think I see. You will know what skills are available? And what skills you need to recruit for. It will also give a clear idea of the taxes you can charge. With this knowledge, it will be harder to hide things from the tax collectors."

I knew this guy was sharp.

"Another announcement is that a new midden is going to be established. The current one is too close to the houses. Rats and other vermin which carry diseases live there. Because it will be further away, Villagers will set their trash outside their door. Trash collectors will pick it up daily. Trash pickup will begin as soon as possible. Those who do not abide by this rule will be fined."

He nodded, and I continued.

"Hog pens will be built near the tannery, and all hogs will be kept there. Any hog found roaming loose may be confiscated by the Barony. Anyone letting another's hog free will be fined or exiled.

"Father, these steps are for cleanliness. A clean village will have fewer diseases. A healthy village works for the glory of God better than a sick one."

I'll probably go to hell for saying this. But it is a message that will be understood in this day and age.

Father Timothy agreed with me.

"I can see that while God gives us trials and tribulations, he also wants us to help ourselves. Keeping our village clean is doing God's work. I will have a sermon about it this Sunday."

"I will be there to show my support."

Whatever my beliefs were or weren't, I had to respect the culture of this time period.

"John, make certain I'm up in time for the first Mass on Sunday."

"Okay, My Lord."

Father Timothy's ears perked up at this unfamiliar word.

"Okay?" He inquired.

I explained its meaning. The Priest repeated it several times, fixing it in his memory.

There was a method to my apparent madness. I will be introducing new concepts which would require new words. Introducing a harmless word up front would make other new ones easier to adapt.

John and I continued to the river. Though fencing hadn't started, a pile of logs was at the starting point. There was a stack of flat stones which the corner posts would sit upon.

Fences weren't built overnight, so this was good progress. As we reviewed the materials collected, two men brought two more fence poles to the collection point. They had one on each shoulder.

I asked them how it was going.

"It is going fine, My Lord. The slowest portion of the job is stopping to sharpen the axes. The blades dull quickly."

I turned to John.

"Do we have extra axes at the Keep?"

"Yes, we do, My Lord."

"Okay then. Have two more be brought to the logging site tomorrow and an extra man to sharpen axes while the others are in use."

"Okay."

While saying nothing, the log carriers were silently mouthing the new word to repeat to others.

"How soon do you think you will be able to start erecting the fence?" I asked.

"We will have enough logs in place to start in the morning. With the extra axes, the loggers should be able to keep up with us."

"Excellent, you men are doing a good job. Please pass that on to the rest of the crew."

No one could say these people weren't quick on the uptake.

"Okay, My Lord."

I had to laugh at that. Slapping the man on the back, John and I went on our way.

As we walked, I shared with him how the smith could make axes that would hold their sharpness longer.

He was doing the right things as far as it went. The Smith was heating the iron and then quenching it. While observing his work, he was tempering the metal with a soak at lower temperatures.

The only thing he needed to do differently was to heat the iron using coal at higher temperatures.

This method would result in a harder wrought iron which would remain sharper for longer.

"Would this work on swords?" John asked.

"Yes, the metal doesn't know what it will be used for, so it will make a harder iron for any use."

By my standards, this was a strange question, but we weren't in my world any longer.

"The Blacksmith will discover this himself now that he can reach higher temperatures with the bellows."

"You don't want to take credit for a better iron?" John asked.

"No, it is best that people be allowed to discover things themselves. It will open their minds to other advances in the future."

I made a mental note to privately show the Blacksmith how to turn iron into steel. I would let him have credit for this finding. A Blacksmith improving iron would be understood by people. Bringing it up out of the blue would open me to witchcraft charges. I had to be careful.

While we talked, we made our way to the Tannery. I had smelled it but had not been there. By choice, I wouldn't visit often.

The Tanner, whose first name I promptly forgot, gave me a tour of his facility.

His work was set up in several stations. The first one was a trimming station where the fresh hide from slaughtered cattle was trimmed and taken to a close stream for cleaning the blood, dirt, and manure from them.

Fortunately, there were no farms downstream. The stream disappeared into a sinkhole, so no problems were created.

The next station was to get rid of hair. The skins would be soaked in an alkaline solution made of wood ash. This way was better than the ancient method of using urine.

The next step would be to scrape off the softened hair and any flesh left. The tanner was proud of his pigeon loft. He used their droppings to soften the hide. This step could take as long as three months, depending on how soft he wanted the hide.

After rinsing the hide again, it would be soaked in a solution made from oak bark. Tanner had an arrangement with the loggers to buy the bark trimmings.

After the soaking achieved the desired color, the hides were placed in a deeper pit and layered with bark. Cold water would periodically be poured over them. This process could take up to a year!

This tour was an example of book learning not translating to real-world experience. I had read about the steps, but until I saw them in action, I couldn't comprehend how dirty this job was and how much physical labor was involved.

In books I had read as a youth, the Indian squaw would chew on the hide to soften it. In my mind chewing was all it took to tan a hide.

By the time the tour was complete, darkness had begun to fall, so John and I headed back to the Keep.

The day had gotten away from me. I had intended to identify a site for a new midden, set up a session on cleanliness with the Midwives, and speak to the Senior Monk about the census being a military secret.

The old saying in my world, "Rome wasn't' built in a day," had nothing on building the twentieth century.

Chapter 10

I had a busy week, following up on all the projects I had underway and starting some new ones. People were accepting the changes, but that might not always hold.

John and I went back to the Tanners area south of the village. This area is downwind of the Village and the Keep for a good reason.

We were looking for a new area for the village midden. I wanted the midden away from the village, so fewer rats were near the houses. Other benefits were reduced odor, and hopefully the wildlife would eat the rats.

The stream that the tanner used disappeared into a sinkhole wasn't the only one in the area. We found one the hard way. I almost fell in.

"Stop!" John yelled.

I stopped and realized I had almost gone over the edge of a sinkhole at least fifty feet deep. It was about fifty feet in diameter and would serve the village's needs for many years.

"Whew, thanks, John. I had no idea I was near the edge."

"I would hate to lose you now. It looks like things will be getting to be fun."

"We will need a trail cut back here for the carts. It shouldn't be too hard. The trail to the tannery comes close, so cutting it out won't be hard."

We would only need a hundred yards cut to the sinkhole. Only three or four trees had to be cut down for a straight road. John will get a work crew out here tomorrow.

While out this way, we scouted for a location to build hog pens. It worked out nicely that there was a flat area next to the sinkhole. The same road could be used for both sites.

The land would need to be cleared for the pens and attached shelters. I asked John to erect a better shelter for those looking after the pens.

Someone would have to be present around the clock, as wolves would try to get at the hogs. Any wolf that got into a hog pen would quickly regret it but could damage the livestock.

The same work crew cutting the trail to the sinkhole could clear the land for the pens. Building pens could be undertaken by the guys erecting the fencing. They should be done by the time the land was cleared.

On returning to the Keep, we stopped at the Cabinet Maker's and confirmed that my chair order had been started. He had all the wood that needed to be cut and dried, so he started to cut and shape wood.

He showed me how he was beginning to shape the legs. I suggested he talk to Fletcher about the device he calls a lathe.

It would be interesting to see where this went. The idea is out there. Will the Cabinet Maker run with it? A lathe would increase its productivity and quality a great deal and would be needed in future metalworking.

Having a full-size lathe would advance things immeasurably. I was taught that the lathe was the first tool that could be used to reproduce itself. All the components for a lathe could be made on a lathe. Try that with a hammer or saw.

I did have one pleasant surprise one evening upon returning to the Keep. The garderobe had been cleaned! When I sniffed the air to see if there were residual odors, there were. Me!

A water basin was kept full of fresh water in my room. I had requested this early on. I'm certain that my daily wash was a topic of conversation in the

Keep. Later I discovered that it was a hot topic in the whole Barony.

The consensus was that the knock on the head upset my humor's balance, leading to this odd behavior. I had no idea what humors were or how they were balanced. I liked that it proved I wasn't a witch. Everyone knew that witches loved filth.

Washing daily with cold water kept me clean, but I missed having a good soak in a tub of warm water.

I decided to commission a copper tub from the Blacksmith. They thought I was odd. A tub would confirm it.

The next day when I described a tub to the Blacksmith and its purpose, he surprised me.

"Some days, my arms or legs get sore. I found that soaking them in warm water heated on this bed of coals smoothed the pain. It would be nice to do this with your whole body."

"The only drawback is that someone has to heat buckets of water."

"That's why God invented apprentices!" He spoke.

Some sayings are ageless.

"I see you have two new apprentices."

"Yes, My Lord, I hope one of them works out. I have found that not all people who think they can smith end up being Blacksmiths."

"You hire two, hoping to get one?"

"I found that to be the best way to end up with a good worker. Some failures run away, some come to me and tell me it isn't working, others I have to tell."

"What happens to them?"

"The runaways are on their own. Two were found dead in the woods by gamekeepers. Some were never heard of again, so they may have made it to another Barony."

He continued, "The ones who come to me, I do my best to get them apprenticed in another trade. Those I have to tell usually either sulk off to their old homes or become lay about in the Village. Those end in being chased out of the Barony or, in one case, hanged. And one may be able to blacksmith – that is, work iron – while the other will be better with copper, tin, or other metals."

This explanation went against everything I had read about the apprentice system, but it made sense. I wondered if this was common practice or if the Blacksmith was a Progressive for this time.

"Is this common practice?" I asked.

"In this Barony, yes. We have found it is best if the workers enjoy or at least don't detest their jobs. From what I understand, not all Barons follow this practice. Occasionally we get a useful runaway from them."

My next order of business with the Blacksmith was the hardening of iron. He reached temperatures of about two thousand degrees by using bellows and coal for fuel. I asked him if he noticed any difference in the metal after quenching.

"It is harder when I first quench it but gets softer with time."

I said haltingly, as though I was thinking of it. "I wonder what cooling it slowly in a warm bath would do."

"It would add to the time to produce a part is what it would do."

"It would be worth it if the hardness remained higher. Tools would remain sharp longer," I said.

"That they would. I guess it is worth a try."

I smiled as I knew it would work. This success would make the Blacksmith more likely to listen to me on other occasions.

I could have stayed and continued this conversation all day. The Blacksmith told me he could have two tubs ready in a week. I must have gotten a funny look when he said, two tubs. He laughed and said, "One for you and one for me."

From the Blacksmiths, I went to the monastery. I had the postponed talk with the Senior Monk about the census being a military secret.

It took him a while to understand that information about the enemies' available resources was necessary for planning a war.

Once he got it, he assured me the tome would be kept under his lock and key. Its existence would be kept secret from most people.

This procedure would have to do. It would be a test of the Senior Monk's loyalty or common sense, if nothing else.

The next item with the Senior Monk was the continuation of teaching Arabic numerals. He completely accepted this change. I told him they were introduced by a group living in the Holy Land.

"God touched, no doubt."

I left that line alone, whatever works. Two monks were summoned.

The first one was Friar Mark. I had rejected him previously. He was now cleaned up and presentable. Relatively so for this period. I smiled and nodded my acceptance. His relief was apparent.

The second one was an average-looking monk. However, I about fell over when I was introduced to Friar Tuck! I kept a straight face with a lot of effort.

Cornwall wasn't Robin Hood territory, nor was this the correct period, so it was just a coincidence.

I hoped.

Using wax slates, I went over the basics of using Arabic numerals. They both were quick on the uptake, so it wasn't like teaching first graders.

I explained that the numbers and shapes were Arabic numerals, and their use was called arithmetic. People who worked with numbers were called Mathematicians.

After about an hour, they could add and subtract any number presented, no matter how high. I promised them that we would take up multiplication on my next trip.

They both had seen the multiplication table I had left and were eager to delve into its mysteries.

Their words, not mine. Wait until they get to division and fractions!

Square roots were far in their future. Then Algebra, Geometry, followed by Trigonometry. If Math were a deep mystery, then Calculus would be, well, I don't know what it would be. Mind-blowing?

On my way to check on the fencing, I noticed a minor commotion on the main village road. A small parade of carts was working their way through my town.

It didn't take long to establish this was the first-grain shipment heading to Saltash. The carts came to a halt as I stood in the middle of the road.

A grizzled-looking man-at-arms was in the lead.

From my dress which was better than the rest and clean to boot, he concluded I was the local Baron.

"My Lord, I was instructed to stop if you appeared. Are you willing to buy our grain at the same price as if delivered to Saltash?"

"I am."

He got a huge smile.

"That makes my job easier."

In the meantime, John Steward came running up. He had been notified of the small caravan's arrival.

I introduced John as my Steward and grain buyer to Sergeant Billings from Wadebridge. I told the good Sergeant that John would take care of the business.

The Sergeant accepted this as normal. All four of his fellow men-at-arms gathered around to listen to the negotiations.

I listened as they established how they would determine how much grain there was. It seemed there was no set of common weights and measures.

If the grain had been taken to Saltash, the buyers in Saltash would have used their weights. They went back and forth for a long time without agreement.

I finally had enough.

"Sergeant, how much did your Lord expect to receive for the grain."

"One thousand and fifty-five silvers".

"Then that is what we will pay this time. In the future, we will have a common set of weights between the Barons."

What the Sergeant hadn't noticed while this negotiation was occurring was that Father Timothy had been talking to the cart drivers and explaining that we would be keeping enough food to feed the entire village through the winter and that they and their families were welcome to join us and become members of our community.

I felt we would gain new people in the Barony from the positive body language shown. It seemed a simple choice, stay and starve, or join us and live.

John and the men-at-arms went to the Keep to collect the silver. The carts were directed to our recently fumigated grain stores. I went with the workers and continued explaining that we were serious about taking in new community members and that there would be food and work for all.

I didn't try to oversell it. Not starving through the winter would sell itself. What I had to think about was housing new people. As it stood, we had three empty houses for families. My discussion with the workers led me to believe that we might need another six houses, and that was for the Wadebridge people alone!

Chapter 11

That evening in the Keep, I nursed a goblet of wine. The stuff is bad, but it is the adult beverage of choice.

I was sitting with a small group consisting of men-at-arms and workers. Mostly listening to get a general idea of the people I was now part of.

They didn't meet any of my preconceived notions. They were intelligent and had a wide knowledge of what was happening worldwide. The men-at-arms were similar in their thinking to soldiers of my time. The workers complained of the same things as all workers. Too much work and not enough pay, and no, you can't have it tomorrow.

One thing, their sense of humor was bawdy! I mean barnyard, down-to-earth bawdy. I tried to imagine them talking on a twentieth-first-century college campus, which boggled my mind.

Of course, they would have fit right in with my World War II Combat Engineers.

I finally figured out how they knew so much about world affairs. Most had never been the proverbial five miles from where they were born. Others had been as far as Saltash, a seaport. It was from there that information was disseminated. Out of date, undoubtedly, but we couldn't affect events anyway.

I noted that I needed to set up an information-gathering pipeline in Saltash and all the surrounding Baronies. We could call it the Cornwall Intelligence Agency. The CIA. What fun.

I could set up the Feudal Bureau of Intelligence if we got large enough. The FBI.

I wondered what Father Timothy would say to name our tax collectors the Infernal Revenue Service. The IRS.

At that, I decided I had enough bad wine and went to bed.

*****

The next morning, with John Steward at my side, I went on a mission I had dreaded. Cook was in the kitchen, and I had to bring up the cleanliness issue.

I went in ready to do battle. Halfway through the door, I stopped in my tracks. The kitchen was spotless. Cook and her helpers were all in clean clothes, and from their shiny faces, they had all washed.

Thinking quickly, "Cook, I want to compliment you on the breakfast and, now that I'm here, the cleanliness of the kitchen and your staff."

Butter wouldn't have melted in her mouth.

"Thank you, My Lord. We try."

"Well done, keep up the good work."

As we left the Keep, I asked John.

"What happened back there? How did she know I was coming to get the place cleaned up?"

"Everyone knows about Father Timothy's sermon and your feelings on the matter. That and how you complimented the Baker on keeping his area clean. She is not dense. They have been working on cleaning the kitchen for the last two days. I'm glad they got it done before you visited."

"So am I. Now we can see if Cook will keep it that way. We will do another walkthrough next week."

"Yes, James."

I took that reply as a sign of approval.

Our first item of the day was to ride out and check how the fencing project was going. It was a pleasant surprise to find that the project would be completed by the end of the day.

That meant the drinking water source would start to clean up, and the workers would be available for other projects.

I talked to each fence builder and complimented them on a well-done job.

We then rode our horses several miles to a prospective limestone quarry. The quarry was on undeveloped land with no farms being close. My Barony was thinly settled and held room for many more farms than existed.

I was encouraged by what we found. A large hillside had been partially washed away to reveal Cornwall limestone, a type of Devonian limestone.

I knew this because I had read a book on types of stone. I mentally opened the page on limestone deposits in Cornwall and found the proper entry.

The large hillside would provide enough limestone for our foreseeable needs. This mine was to be an open pit operation or quarry. We would need workers, tools, buildings to live in, kilns, and roads.

The workers would live on-site because too much time would be lost walking back and forth.

I was forgetting something, but this was enough to start. Oh yeah, kilns need fuel, plus we had to have a water source.

Water proved to be easy. There was a spring-fed stream close by. Part of the project would be to fence in the source area where clean water would be drawn.

That made me think of a midden and nightsoil collection and disposal. No one said this would be easy or could be done overnight.

We could make enough quicklime to make the cement and concrete to build the houses I hoped to need before winter set in, but it would take a year or more to develop the necessary infrastructure.

I could see a small village being developed in this area. That meant a need for schools and other support structures.

The most critical feature in limestone processing is the kiln. Brute labor could quarry the needed limestone. I had already checked to see if anyone had experience building a kiln. Even though it was a well-known technology then, none of my people knew how. That meant I would have to direct the operation.

I would use the most common early kiln, an egg-cup-shaped burning chamber with an air inlet at the base (the "eye") constructed of brick.

Note to self-start clay brick making.

The Limestone would be crushed by hand to fairly uniform 1–2½ inch lumps. Fine stone to be rejected.

Successive dome-shaped layers of limestone and coal would then be built up in the kiln on grate bars across the eye.

Note to self. Need metal grates made.

The kiln would be kindled from the bottom when loading was complete. The lime was cooled and raked out through the base when burnt through. Fine ash dropped out and was rejected with the 'riddling's'.

I couldn't make a note to myself. I missed my Kindle.

Only lump stone could be used because the charge needed to "breathe" during firing. This need to breathe also limited the size of kilns and explained why kilns were all about the same size. Above a certain diameter, the half-burned charge would likely collapse under its weight, extinguishing the fire.

Each kiln makes twenty-five to thirty tons of lime in a batch. Typically, the kiln would take a day to load, three days to fire, two days to cool, and a day to unload, so a one-week turnaround was normal. We would learn the best heats and times by varying the amount of fuel used.

If we could get one twenty-five-ton load this year, we would have enough limestone to build the houses and several other projects. Not enough for a walled village, unfortunately.

Because there were large temperature differences between the center of the charge and the material close to the wall, a mixture of underburned, well-burned, and dead-burned lime would be produced.

A low fuel efficiency, with 0.5 tons or more of coal per ton of finished lime. So to get my twenty-five tons of lime, I would need twelve and a half tons of coal.

Now to find the coal. Finding the coal was easily done as there were several well-known exposed coal seams in the area. It was a shame they were at least five miles from the limestone.

We would start with the known limestone and coal formations but keep looking for ones close to each other. At least until there was so much infrastructure in place, it would be uneconomical to start over.

We trailed over to the closest coal seam. The nag I was riding had an easy gait, but I knew I would be sore tomorrow as it had been many years since I had ridden. Years? Make those centuries!

It was already being worked on a small scale. This is where the Blacksmith sourced his coal. A nearby farmer and his two teenage sons worked the open face of the seam.

The farmer showed me a day's production. Farming was what they did full-time, so the coal was an afterthought. However, the silver they made enabled them to survive winters better than their neighbors.

They were able to do about a ton a week. I needed fifty tons or more, so that would never do. All this coal belonged to me, but I wasn't about to take their means of survival.

"I need a lot of coal soon. More than you and your sons can provide. I will have a crew come in and mine about fifty tons. I'm offering you two pennies per ton we mine from this seam. Is that acceptable?"

It must have been because he was nodding his head like a bobblehead. He never got a word out. His sons were standing there wide-eyed. I had just offered one hundred pennies or ten silver for my coal, and they didn't have to do any work.

They must have thought I was mad!

"Of course, you and your boys can still mine the seam and sell coal when my people aren't working here. This coal arrangement will last until next summer. After that, the coal rights completely revert to me. I'm paying for the immediate coal removal so that even though it is mine, you don't feel like I'm stealing what has been traditionally yours to mine and sell."

"Why would you do that?" He asked.

"You will need the money."

"Why."

"To pay me for your farm, which I'm selling to you."

Now he and both of his sons were making like bobbleheads.

"It's to my advantage to sell you the property. You will have to pay taxes, but everything produced will be yours to sell as you will. When you produce for yourself and your family, I have found that you will grow more than if growing for me. I will be able to lower the tax rate and still have more income."

You could almost see the wheels turning in his head.

"My Lord, if I understand you correctly, you are selling me the farmland I currently use. I will keep the crops and any monies made from them. Since the land also contains this coal seam, you consider it mine and will pay a fee for any coal you remove until next summer, and then it reverts to you."

"You understand correctly. Feel free to tell your neighbors they will have similar opportunities to buy and a temporary share in any resources found on their land. I'm doing this because you will have a better income as Freemen in the Barony than Serfs attached to the land."

I didn't mention wanting to get a money economy going rather than barter.

"What sort of resources, My Lord?"

"Limestone, coal, iron ore, silver, hardwoods, and clay beds come to mind. I will look at anything else that might be interesting."

John and I then rode three miles to the known iron ore location. We left behind an excited farmer and his sons talking a mile a minute.

On the way, I explained to John how a money economy allowed for greater growth. He understood as the town of Saltash worked this way. That is why it was the power in the area.

As I had previously told myself, these people were as intelligent as any of those in the future. They were ignorant, not stupid. And ignorance can be cured.

The iron ore mine was also being mined as an open pit. From the looks of it, it would soon be mined out unless the ore bed widened out considerably underground. We would have to keep searching for more iron ore.

I had the same basic conversation with the farmer whose land held the iron ore as I had with the farmer with coal.

John and I returned to the Keep as the weak shadows were getting long. It would soon be dark on this cloudy November day.

It had been a good day. I had accomplished everything I had set out to do except talk to the midwives about cleanliness. I can't say I was looking forward to that conversation.

Chapter 12

The next week was a little crazy. Most of our farmers had their crops in for the year. So I could hire many of them and their kids for my projects.

Altogether there were seventy-eight new bodies available. Mostly men, a few boys, and two girls. The girls were desperate for work as they were both orphans supporting younger brothers and sisters.

They were hired at the same rate as all the others, four pence a day. One of the girls was big and strapping and could work alongside any man in the Barony. The other looked like a breeze would blow her away.

All the candidates had assembled outside of the Keep. John Steward summoned each one forward and assigned them to a work detail. It was like choosing sides in a schoolyard. The young lady was last and looked panicked. She and her siblings might starve if she didn't get this job.

John didn't know what to do with her.

I whispered to John, "She can be my runner, delivering messages."

"Good idea, James."

Later, John told me that Gloria was fifteen and her sister Ruth was ten. They lived in a pigsty! More accurately, in a lean-to shelter behind the sty.

"I've taken the liberty of moving them into the Keep. They will share a small room off the kitchen," John said.

"Good. Ask Cook if the little girl can be of use in the kitchen. If so, pay her for her work."

We also got our first new citizens of the Barony. Four families from Wadebridge joined us. The Baron there had taken all their grain to sell in Saltash, leaving them starving.

This influx brought to the forefront a problem I knew we would have. We only had three unoccupied hovels in the village. I could have referred to them as houses, but they were hovels!

The fourth family was put up in one of the extra rooms above the stables in the Keep. It would work for now, but it highlighted the need for bricks to build houses.

Five of our workforce were detailed to level an area near a clay bed to be the drying area for the bricks. Most of the moisture had to be removed before we could fire them in a kiln.

The Cabinet Maker had boards that he had rejected for various flaws, and they were used to make the brick molds.

The clay was dug up and picked clear of unwanted matter. It would then be mixed to the right consistency for brick making. Historically, the clay would be tempered by the weather and water underfoot in open pits for two to three days. To speed up the process, we got all the water out of it we could.

Then water would be added to the clay to make a thick paste. The workers would mix it with their feet like stomping grapes. When mixed well, the clay is put into four inches by three inch by eight inch wooden molds to form the shape of the brick.

The open top molds would be placed on a smooth bed of sand in a south-facing field to allow the clay to dry.

When molding a brick, no air can be trapped inside the clay. Excess clay is removed by running over the mold with a wire.

The molds are laid out to dry for two days and two nights, being turned during that time to assist initial drying. The workers then turned them again on edge and stacked them in rows, one on top of the other, to dry. Normally it would be for one to three months, depending on the weather and time of year.

I built a shed for the bricks to speed up the process from months to a week. A fire was kept burning outside, and hot air was blown into the shed by continuously working bellows. Men were rotated to keep the bellows moving. It was the hardest job on the project.

When the bricks are deemed dry enough, they are fettled, trimmed of "flash," and stacked to form a kiln to bake them. Flues are set into the kiln, and wood fuel is then prepared. The fires are lit, and the bricks are "burnt" in kilns containing 800 to 1,000 pieces.

The firing usually takes two to three days to reach the required temperature. The kilns are then allowed to cool naturally for two days. Then they can be dismantled, and the bricks sorted and stacked ready for use.

Since no oxides would be added, the resultant bricks would be white. Future building bricks would be red, but I needed these fast. And the red color was a cosmetic issue and tradition from my time.

Building a five hundred square foot house would take about four thousand bricks. That meant four kilns needed to run simultaneously to build one house.

I ordered kilns to be fired in lots of twenty so five houses could be built at a time. It would take months to create the houses we would need.

Twenty-five workers were detailed in brickmaking. I left it to John to determine which worker would be the supervisor and would get sixpence a day. I thought about teaching the six-pence song but thought better of it.

I explained to the supervisors that brickmaking would be ongoing for the indefinite future. Ideas for improvements would result in bonuses.

This speech added more words and ideas to Cornlish.

As a stop-gap measure, I had two long houses started. These were the same as those made by Native Americans. They didn't take that long to build and would take care of any sudden influx of new people.

If not needed, they could be used as sheltered storage space.

Two more shipments of grain on their way to Saltash arrived late the next morning from

Wendon and Bodmin. The negotiations went smoothly. Word had spread that we would buy grain at market price and save them two to three days on their journey.

This time we even made offers on the better carts and animals being used to haul the grain. The barons sending the shipments must have figured out that I would need them because the prices had been determined in advance.

Again, John did the bargaining. I would have been taken to the cleaners, but I did pay close attention to his tactics.

As before, the cart drivers were approached about joining us. Since they were conveying the food that would have sustained them through the coming winter, I suspected we would see people from their Baronies.

Once their people joined us, I could foresee a lot of trouble in the future as the Barons would accuse me of stealing the people they planned to starve.

I was pleased to see that a rough road had been cut to the new midden. It was already in use. My announcement about fines must have been taken to heart.

It helped that the predecessor in this body was rotten to his people. I regretted his attitude even though I benefited from it.

The nightsoil collection was also underway that week with the completion of the nightsoil collection wagon.

I rode my horse to the new midden and nightsoil collection pit. There was no problem in finding the pits. You could smell them half a mile away, better here than in the village. Reminding me that lime production needed to be started as soon as possible. It would dry things out and keep the stench down.

When the lime was available, it would be spread over the noisome mess, followed by a thin layer of dirt. Several years later, this could be dug up and used as fertilizer.

While in the area, I also checked on the new hog pens. The land was cleared, and stout pens were being built. This work was being done by some of the younger boys who would be stationed here.

Unlike most boys from my time, they were working with a will. After all, they were earning tuppence a day. A small fortune by their standards.

While all my outgoing monies wouldn't dent my treasury, I still had to think of future income to keep things moving.

In line with this, John and I discussed when we should forward grain to Saltash. We decided to accumulate the grain into one shipment. It would be traumatic for the merchants in Saltash to find their prices had gone up. And we needed a strong, guarded presence, so we only wanted to go through this once.

Now that the streets were a loose definition of clean, it was time to talk to the Midwives.

Chapter 13

The five of them were gathered in the Keep one morning. They all showed up because I offered silver for the day. I had Father Timothy and Senior Monk Luke present to avoid future problems.

Being burned as a witch was not in my plans.

Working with the Monks, I made a crude magnifying glass using a hog intestine they had scrapped as thin as possible for me. It wasn't completely transparent, but you could see things through it fairly well.

The intestines were stretched across a frame to keep it taut. The cabinet maker ensured the frame could be adjusted up or down.

A flat piece of metal was burnished smoothly by the blacksmith to act as a reflector. The smith was amazed at the amount of light produced by a candle with a reflector behind it. I think he had a new product to sell.

I placed a drop of boiled water on the intestines creating a crude magnifying glass. A second layer of the film was under the first to act as the sample slide.

This setup gave me an estimated ten-power magnifying glass.

I turned to the midwives. Each was dressed in work clothes to show off how many children they had helped birth. In other words, they were a dirty, smelly mess!

Before I started my lecture, I asked how many of these children survived their first month. One out of three didn't make it. That is why they didn't name the children until they were two months old.

I found this to be emotionally heartrending. My pragmatic side found it to be a waste of manpower. No matter the reason, this had to change.

"What is the smallest thing you can see?" I asked.

One of the ladies cracked, "If it is Agnes, it might be a horse."

All the others laughed, so I guessed this didn't offend Agnes. That reminded me of a basic courtesy I had forgotten.

I introduced myself and then asked their names. As they gave them, I inquired how long they had been Midwives. It varied from five to twenty years.

Agnes was the one with twenty years of experience. She was sixty-four by her best guess and was old by their standards.

Midwifing was a second career for them.

After the introductions, it was agreed that a thin strand of human hair was the smallest thing you could see.

I then had Agnes donate a strand of hair. She was preening at all this attention. Her attitude was a good thing from my perspective. As a senior Midwife, I needed her to buy in.

I guided her into gently laying it on the slide.

Then I lit the candle. The ladies were impressed with the amount of light reflected.

I then asked them to gently squeeze one of their eyeballs.

One of the ladies said, "Just like when we were children and wanted things to look larger?"

"Exactly! Do you know why that works?"

No one had an answer.

"When you look at something close, things far away are faint, or looking far away makes close things fainter. That is because you changed the focal point of the eye.

"When you squint your eye, you change the focal point more than the eye is made for. That is why things appear larger."

There were several nods. Some of them got it. I had a large wax tablet provided by the Monks to make crude drawings. And proceeded to the next step.

I also had to invent the chalkboard.

Explaining that a drop of water acted the same as a squeezed eyeball, I put several drops on the top film.

Then each person present looked through the drop to see the thin hair. I had tested it and knew it would work, but I was still relieved when it did.

Many exclamations were made when they saw how large the hair now looked. So far, so good.

Afterward, I returned to Agnes and asked if I could take a sample from her dress. She was reluctant but allowed me. She had delivered a baby yesterday, so I took the sample from the freshest spots.

This part was a gamble, but it paid off.

"Ladies and gentlemen. Some animals are too small for us to see."

Placing the sample on the slide, I looked and could see large bacteria swarming about. Victory!

149

Each person present looked through the magnifying glass. Someone mentioned dirty Agnes, so I shut that down by taking samples from everyone's clothes, including the guys.

These samples proved that everyone carried these small creatures.

"Like all creatures, these small animals poop. Would you rub poop on a newborn and the mother?" I asked.

Of course, they wouldn't.

I invited Agnes to take a sample of my clothes. She did, and we all examined them. There were only a few bacteria on my clothes.

Agnes was the perfect straight woman when she asked why the animals weren't on me.

"I had these clothes boiled last night in clean water. It killed all the little animals. I call them bacteria from the Latin word for rod, which many appear like."

The holy men smiled. They had known the Latin meaning. The devil wouldn't speak Latin.

Mary spoke up.

"We can kill the animals by boiling our clothes, but we can't boil our hands."

I was waiting for this.

We took a sample from Mary's hands. As expected, bacteria was present.

Then I had her wash her hands with hot water and lye soap. When we looked again, the bacteria were gone. I then had her go around the room and touch things.

Another sample from her hands had the bacteria back. Another washing, and they were gone.

I explained that this demonstrated why hands had to be washed frequently during birthing.

I was so proud of Agnes when she stated that she would have several boiled aprons to wear. She would change them frequently!

The last action of my class was to present each Midwife with an armband with a red cross. I had two more in reserve but didn't know how Father Timothy and Senior Monk Luke would feel about getting a 'woman's' award. From their jealous looks, I hurriedly brought them out.

I explained the red cross symbolized a trained medical person who understood why cleanliness was critical during the birthing process.

As their spokesperson, Agnes, inquired, "Should we insist that the mother be cleaned before she starts to deliver?"

"That is an excellent question, ladies. I should have thought of that. Cleaning the mother is one more step in ensuring that the child lives beyond one month."

After the ladies left, Father Timothy asked if he could write treatises on the magnifying glass and the importance of cleanliness during the birthing process.

Senior Monk Luke asked if he could copy those treatises for general distribution.

"You may copy and sell them, but you must give Father Timothy thirty percent of the profits as the author."

"What about you, My Lord?" Father Timothy asked.

"I want healthy children everywhere."

"Even in other Baronies?" Senior Monk Luke asked.

"They may be mine someday, so yes."

They said nothing, but I had just thrown the cat amongst the pigeons.

John joined us, and we had a quick update on the census. About seventy-five percent of the farms and the village had been counted. The monks had started collating the village information. They expected to have the project completed in the next fortnight.

Chapter 14

The next morning before eating breakfast, I went to the kitchen. I was pleased with how clean the place looked. That was until I opened a cupboard door. It was dirty, with spilled grease catching all the dust.

Cook was behind me and gasped. She rounded on the scullery maids and began shouting. I left quickly. Otherwise, I might end up scrubbing the place down. She was hot!

After eating, I went to the Blacksmith's forge. It was early enough that he hadn't started his day's work.

"Do you have time to talk about steel?"

"I always have time to talk about steel, My Lord."

I had given up on the title thing.

"From my understanding, carbon gives the steel its properties."

"That is correct," the Blacksmith said. "Every apprentice knows that. What we don't know is how much carbon to use\

I told him, "There are three types of steel: low, medium, and high carbon.

"Low-carbon steel, or mild steel, contains under 0.3 percent carbon. It's known for being easier to weld and shape than higher-carbon steels. It's softer and more pliable. Mild steel is the least expensive type of steel and can be used for fencing, pots & pans, and machine parts, to name a few.

"Medium-carbon steel contains between 0.3 percent and 0.6 percent carbon. It offers a balance of workability, price, and durability. Pressure tubing and road plates are common usages.

"Then there is high-carbon steel. This steel contains between 0.6 percent and 2 percent carbon. It's extremely hard and is often used for tools, cookware, and knife blades. However, its hardness can make it more brittle than other steel, and it isn't easy to weld and work after forming."

"That sounds good," the Blacksmith said. "But figuring out the right proportion of something is difficult. It would take all day to figure out the weight and then do the arithmetic."

The arithmetic wouldn't mean anything to the smith he would gauge temperatures by color until accurate high-temperature thermometers could be invented. The biggest labor-saving invention I could recommend to the smith is using a donkey to lift a drop hammer.

I explained, the hammer could be a wooden post with stone to weigh it down and an iron shoe on the part that strikes things. It would vastly multiply the forge's productivity.

"Plus, the Monks at the Monastery have a better way of doing arithmetic. I will have someone show you how to use the new numbers."

"New numbers?" He asked.

"Arabic numerals, they are much easier to work with."

I would also need to develop a standardized system of weights and measures.

From the forge, I walked to the Monastery. The streets were noticeably cleaner than they had been.

The Monks were waiting at the door. I had promised them more arithmetic lessons today, and they were eager.

Today we were working on dividing fractions. We went at it for half an hour before inverting, and multiple began to sink in.

"Why does this work?"

"God has ordained it so," I said.

A safe answer at any time, I didn't want them to know I didn't know.

From the looks exchanged by the Monks, I might be working on sainthood.

That religious thought made me spend several seconds reminiscing how I had gotten here in the first place, but I quickly let it go. I'm here. Nothing to be done but to get on with it.

Luke, the Senior Monk, took me aside.

"These young men have been working hard. Is there any way to reward them?'

I thought for a moment and smiled.

"Yes, we will give them an armband with the addition, subtraction, multiplication, and division symbols to show they have learned the material."

"Friar Luke, do you know the award for success on a hard project?"

He answered with a cautious "No."

"More hard work. These young men will be teachers in the new school."

"What new school?"

"The one where everyone in the Barony will learn to read, write, and use numbers," I said.

"Why do they need that?"

"So we can expand the productivity of the Barony. Just think of all the new customers for your books."

That took him aback.

"When will this school start?" He asked.

"Probably not until winter. We have many things to do, but there will be a school."

What I didn't say was there will be elementary, secondary, and colleges before we are done. No sense in Luke thinking I'm completely crazy.

I returned to the Keep and picked up a horse to visit the new mines and quarry. I had to step aside while hogs were herded to the new hog pens. The boys doing the herding gave me a cheerful wave.

They were earning money and having a good time doing it. Herding hogs didn't seem fun, but what do I know?

Riding my nag was hit and miss. I needed to invent stirrups!

A road had been cut to the coal seam. The seam itself was being worked.

My team had cut away the side of the hill to open the entire face of the seam. 'It's width and height indicated a lot of coal, and we would need a lot of coal.

I asked the supervisor what held up the coal production the most.

"It's not mining the coal that holds us up. It breaks free easily. It's getting the coal to the quarry for making lime, the Blacksmith for his projects, and the iron ore mine."

"Aren't the roads good enough?" I asked.

"Not the best. Rough tracks, but they work. We don't have enough wagons, animals to pull them, or trained drivers."

"I'll see what I can do."

It was a shame the gradient was all wrong. A small stream nearby flowed away from the iron pit. If it had flowed toward it, we could have used it to float boxes of coal, saving a lot of work.

At the limestone quarry, they had fired the first lime kiln. It would be several days before we knew how successful it would be. Everything looked good to me, but I had book knowledge, not practical experience in this area.

I reviewed the materials they had put in the kiln. They used the proper-sized lumps so air and heat could circulate. Now all we could do was wait and see.

The iron ore operation was well underway. The locals had been mining ore in small lots for years, so it was easy to scale up. Throw more men and equipment at it!

The supervisor I had appointed was proud to demonstrate a rock crusher they rigged up. It was a simple vertical chute. A small pony would pull up a weight with an iron boot made by the Blacksmith.

The weight was dropped one or more times, and the ore was crushed to a workable size. The ore was then put in a coal-fired kiln.

I pitied the poor pony!

When I expressed this, I was told four ponies were rotated through the job during the day. It would be foolish to work your animal to death. Once again, I was reminded these people were ignorant, not stupid.

They could make a ton of iron a week at their production rate. I challenged the supervisor to devise ways to make ten tons a week.

Right now, a ton was plenty, but in the next year, the requirements would go up.

On the way back to town, I thought long and hard about how to get more wagons, drivers, and horses. I kept going in circles with no solution in sight.

Until I got back into town and found the solution waiting for me, it was so obvious that I even slapped myself up the side of the head.

Chapter 15

On the road through the village sat a caravan taking grain to Saltash while John was negotiating the grain purchase.

Taking him aside, I asked if we could rent the carts, horses, and drivers for the next three months.

It was surprisingly easy to strike a deal. Since we had enough food in storage from previously purchased shipments to last the winter, they would take the grain to Saltash.

From how the other Baron's guards acted, I suspected some of the Baron's rental money wouldn't make it back. It didn't matter to me. It was their hides at stake.

We had the grain caravan pull to the side of the road and would have to arrange for our men-at-arms to accompany the shipment to Saltash. John would be going with them to conduct the business end of things.

While this was being sorted out, three more groups of wagons pulled in. These wagons were bigger and sturdier than any that had come before. We paid the market price with no quibbling.

Again the wagons were rented to us for the next three months. This equipment windfall would take us until the weather got so bad, we had to suspend operations.

A side benefit was that the drivers we just hired would get a chance to see what we provided to any who joined us.

The next day I returned to the coal seam we were mining. The crew had just built and lit off the first coke oven. I was excited about this.

The coked coal would enable the Blacksmith to make higher-grade steel. The coke would also provide purer carbon from its soot to add to the steel.

We were on our way to producing high-carbon steel. I need high-carbon steel for the new type of crossbow I want to make. It was a variation of the types of crossbows used in my original history.

I was so excited about the crossbow possibility I returned to town to talk to Smith. I don't think he was pleased with me pulling him away from his forge, but this couldn't wait, at least for me.

I had given a lot of thought to the crossbow features that I wanted for my troops. Like any engineer, I could design an elegant solution. The trick was, could it be manufactured?

I explained to Smith that the steel I needed for a crossbow was called 'Spring steel'. Its name came from its ability to spring back into shape after being bent under tension. I haven't tried to explain what a physical spring was yet.

Steel would be used to make the prod, the portion of the bow that was bent back to provide force. It acted the same as a bow stave.

The spanning mechanism would be a winch pulley to draw back the prod. Simple to make and use, it would provide two bolts per minute as a firing rate. This rate was slow compared to an archer but deadly in its effect.

To release the taut prod and 'steel string' used in place of a bow's whipcord string would be a European rolling nut lock. This simple trigger would stand up to field conditions.

The prod would be lashed to the stock or Bridle with a tightly braided rope.

The bolts used would be the traditional four-pointed bolts. These were shorter and heavier than arrows, but could punch through the mail and plate armor.

We would have to experiment with the bolts to see what size and weight gave the best flight trajectory and penetration.

Before that could start, we had to find the right combination of iron, carbon, and silicon to manufacture the Spring steel. Then figure out how much hardening and tempering was needed.

Then I had to talk to the cabinet maker about the manufacture of stocks for the crossbow.

That is all easily said but hard to do.

The Blacksmith and I talked about handling the new project for several days. We finally settled on assigning his best apprentice to the project.

The apprentice, Thad, was easily the largest man I had ever met. He looked as though he could pick up the large anvil and toss it across the forge.

More importantly, he was about finished with his apprenticeship and was known to be a good worker.

Thad would work on this project full-time and would be paid separately. In effect, his apprenticeship was completed. The eight pennies a day I was paying him would have him the target of all the single women in the Keep and village.

There was a small forge inside the Keep that Thad could use, it would hide his work from prying eyes. Thad and Smith couldn't understand why I referred to the small forge as the 'Skunk Works'. I didn't try to explain.

Back at the Keep my bath was finally finished, and I could take a bath for the first time in a long time. It was either a day, centuries, or a lifetime. Take your pick.

I was stopped later that evening by Agnes.

The new cleanliness fanatics talked me into a second small portable bath for bathing mothers before delivery. It was under construction by the Blacksmith.

The midwives would pay for and share it. They even discussed a building to house the bath for other people needing their services. Pregnant women would come to the new building to have their children. Was this to be the first hospital?

The great thing about it was that they thought of this without any hints from me.

The next morning the last grain shipments had come to us, and John led our grain caravan to Saltash.

Now I was waiting for his return.

I pictured every scenario possible, bandits along the way. Being overpowered and robbed by the local Baron. Merchants kidnaping John.

While trying to make the week hurry up, I rode to the new hog pens. They were complete, and the young men watering and feeding them had their lodgings set up.

I hadn't thought much about the housing that would be provided, but someone had. The boys were settled in a small log house that would resist the harshest weather. They had a goodly supply of firewood and were gathering more.

They gave me a tour of their area. They had enough food to supply a medium-sized army, or ten growing boys.

I examined the cesspit that was being used. Each day's contents were covered with a layer of lime, then another thin layer of dirt. The lack of flies demonstrated its success. There was an odor but nothing like before.

A hut had been built on the site to protect workers from getting caught in the rain. Village workers had erected a fence around the cesspit so that animals wouldn't wander into it.

Three of them were making a 'delivery' while I was there. I asked them how things were going.

"Fine, My Lord, this is the easiest work I have ever had, and the other people in the village appreciate it. The only drawback is I have to wash in the river before going home."

I agreed that seemed to be a hard condition of returning home, but what was a man to do? Happy wife, happy life.

From how he and his partner laughed, I knew I had introduced a new phrase to this time and place.

"Where did you get those armbands, you are wearing?" I asked.

"We decided if the Midwives had a marker, we deserved one also."

"I agree and should have thought of it myself. I like that it has an outline of the village to show you work for the village."

"Speaking of working for the village, we need to get back to work."

At that, two men began dumping waste pots into the cesspit. The third stood there and watched.

I had the first village road crew!

John finally returned with bags of silver.

He had negotiated a thirty-five percent price increase. This increase paid for the grain we had stored for the winter and the teamster rentals.

As Father Timothy put it, the Bishop was now paying for the poor's daily bread.

And the poor were coming. New people were arriving at the village daily.

We set up a reception center of sorts for them. It was a Bench in the village square manned by Monks. As people arrived, they were interviewed about their jobs and added to the local census.

My red cross-wearing Midwives checked them over for any obvious signs of disease. Only one person was isolated for a while, but we were lucky it was only some form of the flu.
Each person was assigned to one of the long houses we had built. Single men and women were in two separate houses, and families in a third. They were also given a meal token which showed they were registered and now considered citizens of my Barony.

The first houses with the new bricks were going up. We held a lottery to see which families would get the first of the ten houses completed. Some villagers complained about the newcomers getting the best houses.

I told them everyone would get a new brick house, but it would take most of the winter to build them.

Anyone complaining would move to the back of my list.

I didn't have a list, and one wasn't needed. The whiner shut up.

One of the projects I had started, a town laundry, was completed. Clothes were cleaned in boiling water and soap rather than rinsed in the river.

The next public building would be a bath. That would be a culture change. Fortunately, there were enough stories about the Romans that shouldn't be too hard to sell.

My fellow citizens were easier to be around these days. No nasty smells or continuous scratching for fleas.

An occasional farmer would come to town that hadn't bought into the new cleanliness standards. They were told in no uncertain terms to clean up their act!

My chairs had been finished, and my aching back appreciated them. It became bragging rights for the locals to say they had sat in one of the new-fangled chairs.

The Cabinet Maker was overwhelmed by the orders that came in. In several months you could go into one of the hovels in the village and see a chair sitting in pride of place. Many times, it was the only piece of furniture.

The new Monk teachers had their first students. I called the lessons night class because they took place early evening. They couldn't be real night classes because the area was sound asleep come dark.

The students were mostly local craftsmen, like the Blacksmith and the Cabinet Maker, who saw the utility of the new learning. It was wild one evening when I passed the Monastery gates and heard cheering.

They had figured out how to calculate square feet in a building. It wasn't really in feet since still used hand spans, another reminder that I needed to develop uniform measurements.

My kitchen walk-throughs were over, they weren't needed anymore. The last time I checked the kitchen, Cook was giving tours to local housewives to show off her healthy kitchen.

I loved it and had John give her a five-silver bonus.

Good news kept coming. The Midwives had delivered five children this past month, and they were all alive and well at the two-week mark.

Normally two of them would have died from some form of infection.

Winter was approaching rapidly. More people were arriving daily from other Baronies and the new arrivals were quickly put to work erecting new longhouses.

Chapter 16

The mines and quarries were producing materials in ever-increasing amounts. We had a small stockpile of coal growing daily. The iron ore was keeping up with the Blacksmith's demands.

Where we were falling behind was in lime production. Part of the problem was the limestone quarry. Its working face was too narrow and throwing more manpower at it wouldn't overcome the bottleneck. There wasn't enough room at the face to increase production.

Explosives would have solved the problem, but those were a long way away in our development.

There was another limestone deposit several miles from the one we were working on. It would hurt to open it up as duplicate facilities would need to be built.

I surveyed the new limestone site to ensure the working face was wide enough.

It would work for the building lime we needed.

Building lime is created by adding water and sand to quicklime.

The quicklime was hauled to where we were building houses. Where the quicklime, sand, and water were mixed in a deep container.

The workers would mix the building lime with water then gradually add sand and stir thoroughly. The end product would be a simple cement mixture.

Apply it to bricks and leave for a week, and the bricks are stuck together!

It took many hours of experimentation to get the proper texture, even though I knew the formula for the cement. Most of this was due to the lack of standardized measurements. I really had to do something about that.

A standard measurement for temperature was easy to define. The centigrade system was natural for this. Boiling water would be 100 degrees C, and water at its freezing point would be 0 degrees C.

All we had to do was to mark gradients on our thermometer. It would be a long tube with a hollow glass bubble at one end and a narrow opening at the other.

Heating the air in the bubble with the open end in water would pull water up the tube. The tube would be marked with the temperature gradient. Crude but sufficient.

All I needed was glass.

The only problem was we currently couldn't make glass. Making glass was known in this period, but none was produced in Cornwall.

Glassmaking was simple: heat sand to over seventeen hundred degrees centigrade. When it cools, the silica in the sand will fuse, making glass.

We couldn't reach that temperature, so we had to add potash and quicklime to the mixture. These additions would lower the melting point to under six hundred degrees centigrade, which we could achieve with coked coal and bellows.

But nothing is as easy as it sounds. The first glass resulting from this mixture wouldn't be useable for forming. There was still contaminate left in the glass. This glass was called cullet. We would have to remelt the cullet at least five times to get a glass that we could blow to form tubes.

After manufacturing the first useable glass, future batches could start with purified glass and thirty percent sand, potash, and quicklime.

The molten glass would then be poured into a mold, a metal tube sawn in half lengthwise. The two halves would be combined with clamps while the glass was poured.
A metal rod down the center of the metal tube allowed a glass tube to form. The lower end of the metal contraption would have a bulb, and the metal rod a corresponding bulb.

The Blacksmith had a heck of a time working this out, but he got it done. He only had to make one, as the mold could produce thousands of glass thermometers. I could see the day when thermometers would be a major export.

Working out how to properly melt the glass and produce a usable thermometer took most of the winter. It was extremely crude by my standards, but it worked.

Glass quickly replaced the slides on my homemade microscope. The next step would be to grind glass to the proper angles for microscopes and telescopes. These would have to wait as I had so many items on my to-do list.

The length was the hardest to figure out. There was no way for me to figure out the metric meter. I was stumped for several days until I remembered an odd science project from grade school. We had to measure our pinkie fingers. Mine was .01 meters!

While far from the preciseness of the true measurements, it would give a uniform measurement that was approximate enough to work with.

The Blacksmith must have thought I was crazy with the things I was having him build, but he soon saw their usefulness.

I didn't come up with these ideas in a vacuum. I kept Father Timothy, and Abbot Luke informed each step of the way. Not being burned for witchcraft was still on my not to do list!

Word had come back that the Senior Monk was acceptable as the new Abbot. The bishop sent his reply with the note saying he had prayed over this decision many times. I bet he counted my silver many times too.

Balance scales that could be tared were in common use. For weights, we had to make a container whose inside dimensions were one thousand cubic centimeters and fill it with water heated to four degrees centigrade. That much water was one kilogram.

The kilogram had to wait until we had the thermometer, which depended on glass production.

I didn't spend that much time on weights and measurements. The glass had taken all my spare time.

I say spare time because my real work was with Tom.

Thomas Smith and I were working on Spring steel. I knew the proportions but didn't know the purity of the silicon and iron from which we were trying to make the steel.

There was a lot of trial and error. Mostly error. Tom would melt silicon and carbon in his iron to make a steel bar. He would bend the bar to see if it would spring back. When that didn't work, he would try another random mix.

I introduced him to scientific principles. Once he started keeping notes on the proportions of iron, carbon, and silicon, it made a difference. He tracked time, roughly measured, and color. He would heat the iron billet in the coals to the right color, roll it in sand, hammer it, repeat.

He had tried thirty-two different variations in his first test. After noting down what he had tried, it only took another fourteen times to be able to make a usable spring steel.

Then it was finding the right ratio for crossbow length to prod width. We built several prototypes with the Cabinet Maker's, Mark Woodson, help. They were at the armory's middle and extremes of the old-style crossbows. We figured they wouldn't be too far from what we needed.

We were correct in our thinking and had a working crossbow just after the New Year celebrations. After that, it only took a week to find the best weight and length for the bolts.

I think Tom may have been offended when I showed him how I wanted the crossbow to be manufactured instead of letting him figure it out.

All the parts would be interchangeable.

I had him make up parts for fifteen while Mark made up the stocks. Like the metal parts, the stocks had to be interchangeable. So instead of pounding on metal or carving on wood, they had to continuously take measurements to ensure the parts were the same. And before that, they had to make the measuring tools and jigs that would be used to make those measurements.

To do this, they used the first crossbow that was fully satisfactory, took it apart, measured all the bits and pieces, and fabricated the measuring tools accordingly. If it were an exact fit on the prototype and an exact fit on the copy, it would work.

It was amazing how a simple crossbow had to be measured from so many different angles!

In the middle of January, I had John Steward select ten men to be trained on the crossbow. Within the first week, they could operate the crossbows and hit their targets ninety percent of the time.

Their rate of fire was only two per three minutes, so I insisted that they practice until they could fire twice in one minute. The practice improved the muscles it took to wind the windlass and steady the crossbow. It took until the end of February to reach that goal.

All the additional practices had increased their accuracy to ninety-eight percent. The other two percent I wrote off to random chance.

I now had ten trained crossbowmen that could take on twenty charging Knights. And none of the adjacent Barons had twenty Knights. In all the six surrounding Baronies, there were only thirty-nine known Knights.

The school for all the children of the Barony had been opened after winter. Those that lived on farms stayed in empty longhouses.

A divider was built inside to keep the boys and girls separate. A Matron and a Dean were appointed to live with the separate sexes to keep things down to a dull roar.

Regular inspections became necessary when a tunnel dug between the boys' and girls' sides had been found. Officially I had to frown on it, but I wanted to know which boy had the initiative and leadership ability to make that happen.

It turned out it was one of the girls!

I interviewed her and found her to be a sixteen-year-old, tough-minded young lady. I don't know what she thought the interview was about, but she offered to have my child.

Though not unattractive, Sara Farmer wasn't what I was looking for. Until she offered it, I didn't even realize I was looking.

I explained to the disappointed young lady that I needed someone to lead an auxiliary to the men-at-arms. I wanted her to pick twenty healthy young ladies and lead them to become a support group.

They would help dig fortifications, haul supplies, and help fight if needed. They would be trained in spears and crossbows.

She liked that idea and accepted the position. John Steward was taken aback about having to train young ladies in warfare but did his best.

I figure half would be pregnant and married in four or five months.

I saw our first battle three months or less away, so it worked.

The monks taught in our schoolroom, the front of the longhouse. Unlike the schools I was used to, these students worked hard. Harder than I had ever seen before.

Abbot Luke explained it to me.

These children were being given an opportunity that most noble children never had. Any child that slacked off would receive a beating at home. Any that sassed their teachers would catch it both at school and home.

One father from an outlying farm made the journey to town to beat his son after he found he was making trouble and doing poorly in his lessons. That reinforced the idea to all children that they had better behave and get good grades.

I could only remember a few lines from a song, but 'reading, writing, and rithmatic taught to the tune of a hickory stick' stuck out. That was our school. The students went from first grade to fifth-grade levels in the three months of winter.

After that, they had to go home to work on the farm, but I now had the foundations of a literate society.

My spy operation wasn't as sophisticated.

I hired three single men who were good at miscellaneous trades to travel through each of the six Baronies. They would spend a good amount of time in various ale houses, learning about the local Barons, their families, and the armed forces. Once they had information about them, they would move on.

Along the way, they would learn about local travel conditions and what resources were being used. Most important was how the people fared with grain sold out from under them.

When all the reports were put together, it was apparent that only one Baron was starving his people. The others had them on short rations, but they wouldn't starve.

Baron Wendon would likely invade this spring as his Barony was now in the most trouble.

I had my spies take a more in-depth look at his lands. I wanted to know what roads could be used, natural ambush spots along the way, and if we had to fight in an open field, the best location for our battle.

Chapter 17

While my scouts were finding the lay of the land and the best places for military action, there was enough to keep me busy.

The crossbow squad was progressing nicely and included a support group with war hammers. When fighting in the open, you had to clean up the battlefield.

I had learned that lesson the hard way in Argonne Woods. Leaving a cluster of wounded soldiers would be an obstacle that could cause problems later. Better to neutralize them all.

Killing like this would seem harsh to soldiers of the twenty-first century, or at least to the REMFs. They would pull the wounded off the battlefield and provide medical care. For those of us blooded in Europe and Korea, it was common sense to end them.

The ladies that formed the auxiliary force were trained in a lighter crossbow. Their primary mission would be to defend the village and Keep while the army, small but an army nonetheless, was on the move.

Then there was the Keep itself. That name was a joke compared to the Norman Keeps of later years. My Keep consisted of a large, thatched roof hall attached to a three-story tower. The tower was fitted block, and no one knew its history.

All other operations were in small outbuildings. The kitchen, forge, armory, and others were haphazardly built and placed around the main hall.

The land the Keep was built on was perfect for my needs. The small complex sat on a flat area on top of a hill, about one hundred yards by two hundred yards in size.

I still couldn't wrap my head around the new metric system I introduced for standard measurements. I understood it, but in my head, it would always be inches, feet, yards, and miles.

I had to break this habit, or I would be in battle, hesitating to decide while I converted yards to meters. Not good.

It was time to upgrade the keep. I had a rectangle laid out around the perimeter of the flat to outline where the walls would go. It would take months, but we had enough cement stockpiled to make concrete walls.

First, a foundation had to be dug and then poured. A forge was dedicated to making nothing but rebar to reinforce the concrete.

The forested area east of the village had been cut down to make forms for the walls when we were ready to pour. The stumps were being pulled out so we could farm the area.

Stump removal was brutally hard work in the winter. No one went hungry, but we were wet and cold. Experience taught me that people could and would endure hardship if they thought they were working toward the common good.

Spirits were high. Everyone had enough to eat and was getting paid in silver pennies. What was there not to like?

Another project was digging a well inside the new walls.

Once our dowser identified the best spot, I built a shelter over the site, similar to picnic shelters in parks. The roof would keep the area somewhat dry for the workers and prevent the walls of the well from caving in.

I didn't believe that dowsing worked, but I wasn't going to go against local superstition. I had enough problems explaining real science.

Digging a deep well is not as easy as one might think. The well had to be dug by hand. No drilling rigs here. And it wasn't as simple as digging a hole in the ground and putting a little building on top.

The key to a good well was a good lining to keep groundwater out. Groundwater is what it sounds like. Water seeps into the ground from a rainstorm.

Bacteria from things like uncontrolled dumping of human waste could contaminate water near the surface.

What we needed to do was dig down to an aquifer that was protected from groundwater by a layer of impervious clay.

We would dig a hole the desired diameter and then dig down until we passed through a layer of clay. From there, it was digging until the water was reached.

We were lucky the clay was only fifty feet down, and an aquifer was twenty feet below. While fortunate in the find, the local geology supported its existence.

Buckets and ropes were used to haul the dirt out. When water was reached, it was bailed out as much as possible.

The water didn't rush to fill the hole immediately as the workers bailed it continuously, hoisting the water out with buckets.

The goal was to extend the hole below the waterline allowing the well to produce more water.

The drier we keep the hole, the deeper we can go and the more water the well will produce. When it got to the point where the men couldn't keep the hole dry, they laid stones three feet high around the bottom perimeter.

Then wood forms were placed around the interior of the well and concrete was poured. Each section was allowed to cure for two days before pouring another.

A four-foot wall around the open well was built to keep children and animals from falling in. While building the wall liner, we inserted iron bars to act as steps if someone needed to go down into the well. Most likely to retrieve some teenage showoff. Some things were universal.

Originally, I had thought of having a 'wishing well' roof built to keep out rainwater. Instead, the large canopy was left in place. It was built strong enough to last for many years.

Without my input, concrete benches and tables appeared under the canopy and a new community center was born.

There was no real way to test the flow rate of the new well other than using it heavily. I had a crew of boys haul buckets of water out one after another for two days. The boys worked in shifts day and night and the buckets kept coming up full, so I declared the well a success. It could provide enough water to the Keep while under siege.

My next big project was to improve farming. The current practice was a two-field rotation. A field would be planted one year and left fallow the next.

The fallow field would be used for livestock replenishing the field with poop. This type of crop rotation method worked well as far as it went, but we could do much better.

I called a meeting of the leading farmers to explain my ideas. Farmers are about as set in their ways as any group in the world. Selling new ideas wouldn't be easy.

To soften them up we demonstrated the moldboard plow the Blacksmith had made for me.

Fortunately, horse and oxen collars were commonly used, so ropes around their necks didn't choke the animals. This improvement was less than a hundred years old.

The moldboard plow I introduced had a high-carbon steel plowshare. The moldboard, used for lifting and turning, was made of wrought iron and polished on the upper surface to prevent clogging.

It had a wheel at the front, a high-carbon steel colter to break the soil open, and the wrought iron moldboard to turn the earth after the plowshare cut it to the proper depth. Sorry, Mr. Deere, you will have to prosecute for patent infringement in about a thousand years.

The farmers took turns plowing a furrow with the new plow. They all agreed that it was an improvement and wanted one.

I couldn't wave a magic wand to demonstrate crop rotation though. I thought about explaining how plants used the sun's energy to grow. They already understood they needed sunlight, just not why.

Chlorophyll was beyond my ability to explain. The need for nitrogen was recognized, not nitrogen or how it interacted, but that something in animal waste was good for the soil, thus, good for the plants.

Rather than try to blunder my way through an explanation of the science, I went right to the heart of the matter.

"A better way to rotate crops is to use a four-field method. The first-year field one will have wheat, field two turnips, field three barley, field four in clover.

"The second-year field one turnip, two barley, three in clover, four wheats. The third-year field one will have barley, field two will be planted in clover, three wheat, and field four will be used for turnips. The fourth-year field one has clover, two wheat, three turnips, four barleys.

"Using this method, no field will ever lie unused, and your crop yields will improve."

I was informed that one, I was crazy if I thought that would work. Two, everyone knew fields needed rest. Three, what they were doing wasn't broken, and they weren't going to fix it!

So much for softening them up!

Other than that, they held no opinion on the matter.

One encouraging thought was they weren't afraid of an unreasoning reaction. They had learned I would listen. This attitude was good.

The only way I could win this argument was to demonstrate that it worked. This demonstration would take four years, but it had to be done.

Since spring planting was about to get underway, I had a block of good land selected in each of the quadrants of the Barony. This way, each area could watch my project. Two hundred acres were plowed with the new plow boards. Four fields of fifty acres would be planted as I described.

After four years, I would have harvested half as much as the entire Barony. If that didn't convince them, nothing would!

Even though the winter was almost over, people from other Baronies kept straggling in. Seeing their emaciated bodies made you cry, especially the children.

There weren't many children. When I asked why I was informed they were always among the first to die, along with the elderly.

All we could do was feed and clean the survivors. The village projects completed over the winter were a bathhouse and laundry facility. The two buildings shared hot water.

Coal was used to keep the fires burning day and night. Keeping people and their clothes clean reduced our Barony's death toll to unheard-of levels.

We had five deaths that winter, two from old age, two from logging accidents, and one from a teenager trying to prove he could wrestle a bear. He lost.

I hadn't known that a bear was captive in the woods for such contests. Since the bear had killed a human, I had it put down. That proved to be an unpopular move, but they would get over it. The man who kept the bear was forced into the coal mine.

The hot water also kept things clean. I had all the equipment in the brewery sanitized. It was boiled within an inch of its life.

Once the equipment was cleaned and pure spring water was introduced, the quality of our beer improved greatly. The improvement was good and bad. Good for the taste and bad because so much more was drunk.

On my daily rounds, a stop by the Blacksmith found him proudly showing how he and Mark Woodson had finally come up with foot-powered bellows. Now he could get a blast of air when he wanted it, not when some dimwitted apprentice felt like it.

The Abbot came to me for help. His people had a hard time carving sufficient letters for useful printing.

I led him through a method by letting him discover each step himself.

"So, you want to make many copies of the same letter. How does the blacksmith make many copies of something?" I asked.

"He pours hot metal into a mold."

"Why can't you do that?"

"The clay mold breaks each time," the Abbot said.

"So, you will need many molds?"

"Yes."

"How can you make many molds easily?"

This was the critical question. The Abbot thought for a moment.

"We could press one of our existing letters into the clay, making a mold. We could make many molds and then pour them to have metal letters for impressions, which would last much longer."

Keeping a straight face, I replied, "Brilliant thinking!"

The Abbot left pleased with himself. He had come up with a solution without the help of the young Baron.

Chapter 18

Over the winter, I had an elementary geographical survey of my lands completed. The result was a rough map of the Barony, which had the village, Keep, farms, rivers and streams, forests, roads and trails, and mining sites laid out.

The scale was terrible, but it would have to do until crews with surveying chains could be sent out. I had a 'sandbox' made with all these features using one of the Keep's outbuildings. John Steward and I spent many hours at the table trying to figure out the best siting for our many projects.

One project that was easily put in place was a lumber mill. Not as one would think of a modern lumber mill with giant spinning blades.

The lumber mill would be a bucksaw and pit operation. Tom, the Blacksmith, made two twelve-foot bucksaws for me. One was for use, while the other one was being sharpened.

A log would be set in a trough that extended across a pit ten feet deep. The trough had a slit for the saw blade in the middle of its bottom. A frame was built along one side of the slit to set the cut slab thickness. A log would be pushed slowly along the trough while two guys worked the saw. One above the pit and one poor soul down below.

When I specified a pit ten feet deep, I said nothing about a ladder or steps. I wanted them to get used to figuring these things out for themselves. I should have known better. When I mentioned the pit's depth, I was asked if steps or a ladder were preferred.

"Use your best judgment."

The one down below had all the sawdust fall on them, and their arms would tire rapidly. It took six men rotating between positioning logs, pushing logs through the trough, and the two saw positions.

They could do two three-feet-in diameter, ten-foot-long tree trunks in a day. It was brutal work, and I paid a small premium for it.

Once a tree trunk had been sectioned, cuts were made to square the rounds and clear the bark. A standard thickness of ten lengths, four inches wide and two inches thick, was set. Appropriately these were called two-by-fours.

I really couldn't get my head wrapped around using the metric system. I had been in the US Army for too many years. Not that the Army didn't use metrics; I guess it's better to blame it on my age or, rather, my former age.

A second lumber mill was set up to make larger pieces of wood, like plywood, that would be used in the future. Nails weren't a problem as Smith had been making them for horseshoes all his life.

This was the first task for his apprentices. The apprentice ranks kept growing. At this point, he had five on staff that had proven out.

My intention for the new enlarged Keep was to have concrete outer walls two feet thick reinforced with rebar. The interior would be a large two-story hall. The hall would have two stories of rooms built around its perimeter. These would be of wooden construction using cut lumber.

As it was now on the verge of spring and the new growth of rushes had emerged, I replaced all the rushes in the current Keep.

Previously the rushes had been scattered on the floor so that people wouldn't slip and slide on the flagstones. Rosemary, mint, and thyme would be scattered and crushed underfoot to alleviate the foul smells from spilled food, drink, dried mud, and dog poop.

Instead, I had them weave the rushes into a carpet. It was nothing like a modern carpet but could still be swept clean. It was a full-time job for two widows with children to keep the place swept up, but that was money well spent.

The armsmen soon learned to clean the mud off their boots. It only took the cleaners beating several of them with the brooms to train them.

Watching the older ladies chase a strapping young man and beat him with a broom because he had drug in mud was funny.

You could tell whether a new addition to the castle staff was liked. If the new person weren't liked, they wouldn't be warned to clean their boots. It didn't take many beatings for them to get the message.

I tried to think of this in a twenty-first-century context. No luck.

It didn't take long for the new rush carpets to become common in the village and the more prosperous farms. A new trade emerged, carpet weaving. Weaving was a hand operation. I wondered how long it would be before better looms would be invented.

I hoped I didn't have to introduce them. The more invented by the people, the less chance of me being burned alive!

I went to each test farm to see how things had progressed. With these farms, I would be the largest farmer in the Barony. I suppose I already was because all the land was mine, and the people on farms were all bound to the land. These serfs are only a fine line above being slaves.

I wanted to change that by selling the land to the farmers so that they would be more productive. We would be a food powerhouse with the new equipment and methods I introduced.

Before it was over, I suspected I would have a trading fleet to haul grain to the large markets.

The test farm fields were well underway. They would be ready for spring planting. Local farmers watched the preparations as I went from field to field.

I stopped to talk to some of them, and all the conversations were the same.

"Are you ready for the spring planting?" I asked.

"Yes, My Lord."

"Good. What do you think of what we have done so far?"

"I wish I could afford one of those plow things your men are using. I could double the acreage I plant."

"I'm starting a new program where you can use the new plowshare for a portion of your harvested crop," I said.

"How large of a share?"

"Would five bushels of grain be fair?"

"More than fair, My Lord."

"Then that's what it will be. I will have the Smith make up more moldboard plows and have them available at each test farm."

Nothing was ever easy. I then had to arrange for a person at each test farm to loan out the plows. They had to be able to read and write to keep records of who had what.

Each test farm would have housing for a small crew to watch over the fields. Which meant a better building was needed for a farm supervisor and their family.

Late in the morning, a rider caught up with me. A group of armed men was coming from Wendon!

I was as far from the trail to Wendon as you could get and immediately headed for the Keep.

When I arrived, my small army had gathered. A small packtrain of provisions had been put together to accompany us in the field.

Logistics, logistics, and logistics were what I learned in the US Army.

The lady's contingent was formed and ready to defend the village and Keep in our absence. The wall around the Keep area was only halfway to completion, so that it would be of little help.

As the saying goes, you don't fight with the army you want. You fight with the one you have. That is also true of fortifications.

I think we have a very good chance of stopping this invasion. Worse case, we will weaken them so badly they can't take the Keep.

My five scouts were mounted and rotating in and out of the field with updated information on Baron Wendon's progress. One was staying in contact with Wendon, the others relaying his progress.

Baron Wendon wasn't very organized, and his travel was slow. This dalliance allowed us to arrive at my chosen battle spot and get set up.

We didn't go charging off willy-nilly. My twenty-five footmen and ten crossbowmen marched off at a measured pace. Our pack train followed behind.

The spot I had chosen for the battle was only a one-hour march from the village. Let the Baron's army do the work and tire itself out.

We were on the top of a slight rise overlooking a small meadow with a stream meandering through it.

Four of my men blocked the stream with prepositioned branches and clay as it left the meadow. The water would back up, not enough to flood the field but enough to make it soggy.

It would make it hard going for his men as they charged. Once out of the field, they would run up the hill. The rise wasn't enough to alarm Wendon but would be enough to tire his troops even more.

Near the top of the rise, I had a field of three-inch caltrops scattered. Three paths through the field were marked for my men to retreat. As they pulled back, they were to pull the marking stakes.

But being new troops in their first real battle, I hadn't planned on them remembering to pull the stakes in the heat of their retreat.

We arrived at the battle site well before the Baron's army. One could quibble that neither of us had an Army, only a small group of soldiers.

Even soldiers were a misnomer as there had been little formal training. The exception was the crossbowmen. They had been training for months.

Call it what you want. We were ready to do battle.

Since we were in place well before Wendon and his men, I had the men rest and a light meal prepared. I didn't want them lethargic from a heavy meal. Also, stomach wounds and food don't go together. I didn't bring that up.

Being there early gave me a chance to have armbands passed out. These were to identify our men to each other. Without these, they looked like they could be on either side of the coming fight.

I had a banner tacked to a spear. It wasn't much of a banner, just a blue piece of cloth. My Barony didn't even have a coat of arms. I would have to remedy that. Maybe a dragon on a red and gold field.

Nah, too close to King Arthur of legend. Hmm, it would be nice to know if it was a legend. Anyway, I wasn't going to tempt fate by taking on his trappings.

After an hour, Wendon's men finally came into sight. They stopped on the far side of the stream and milled about for a while.

Finally, a rider broke from the crowd and approached us, waving a small white flag. It may have been a handkerchief.

I advanced through the caltrop field and met him halfway down the rise.

The rider was Baron Wendon himself.

The way he sat on his horse, I didn't think he was completely sober. All good.

"Owen-nap. You are to surrender to my Knights immediately."

"Why should I do that?" I asked.

"To save your life. I will let you ride free if you tell your men they are now mine and the Barony belongs to me."

"Pass."

From the confused look on his face, he didn't understand what I meant.

"To be clear, I will not surrender to your forces," I said.

"Then prepare to die as my Knights charge."

"Can't wait."

It was fun messing with him. From what I saw, this wouldn't be much of a fight.

It wasn't. The Baron's knights went down as they charged into the crossbowmen. Men with war hammers finished them off.

This action must have seemed overwhelming to the Baron's remaining troops.

If they had looked harder, they would have seen that they still outnumbered us, but seeing the Baron and his Knights go down took the heart out of his small army.

A few tried to continue the fight but were taken down as individuals rather than as a cohesive fighting force.

As the battlefield was cleaned up, Knights looted, and caltrops retrieved. We then prepared to advance to Wenden Barony.

I was proud to note that all the caltrop field markers had been pulled up as planned.

Chapter 19

The taking of the Keep at Wendon and my conversations with the Baron's widow went well.

I inquired as to their food reserves. It was a good thing I asked because there weren't any. That was one of the reasons the late Baron had attacked me.

Not to feed his people but to steal my grain to sell to pay for troops.

Since we had goodly grain stores, I arranged weekly deliveries until their harvest could come in months from now. The death rate would have been horrendous.

I also detailed a messenger to her father in Saltash explaining her change in circumstances. The message was to ease the Saltash family's minds before they heard it from another source and to present it as a fait accompli on my part.

I expected he would be jubilant with this turn of events. His daughter was safe, and his grandson would inherit the title.

It would be good to have an ally in Saltash, especially one in trade.

I had to keep reminding myself that language can create the wrong impression. Even though I was looking at the reality of the former Baron's 'Keep', the words that I heard and used in my curious mental translation program created the picture of a Norman Keep.

Nothing could be further from the truth. Wendon's 'Keep' was only a little different from mine. It was a large stone block hall with a two-story 'tower'. My tower was three stories!

I intended to change my Keeps to the late middle-ages style, using concrete rather than all stone. Making them almost impenetrable to current warfare methods.

I say almost because enough time, men, and determination took down the sixty-foot walls of Constantinople. That and gunpowder.

So, without saying 'never', they would be pretty darn strong. Dory hated me swearing. She is dead and gone, who knows where, but she still influences my life.

Another thing that language was messing up with was the titles used. If I remember correctly, the titles in use were Jarl and Thane. I hadn't read that much history of this era, so that I couldn't pull up the book pages in my mind.

The automatic translation used Baron, Count, Duke, and King. I suspected there were others I hadn't been introduced to yet.

Thus, I had a glorious mismatching of terms and titles. Thankfully I didn't have to explain it to anyone from the twenty-first century.

After leaving a group of my men to ensure my victory remained a victory, we returned to Owen-nap.

The village headman and his wife accompanied us. I wanted to start changes in Wendon as quickly as possible.

I didn't try to talk to or convince the couple that the improvements made were for the better. Letting them see for themselves would do the convincing.

I did discuss with John the state, or more accurately, the lack of a state of the road. It would be better to describe it as a wilderness trail. It was only a step above an animal trail in the forest.

"John, I would like you to direct a surveying team to plot the best route for a new road."

"Certainly. What exactly do you want?"

"The straightest road possible. It will have a gentle grade, though this area seems fairly flat. Also, good drainage. Bridges or at least stone fords.

Milestones and pull-off areas for groups to pass each other. And trim the forest along the road so bandits can't ambush people."

"Aye, My Lord, will tomorrow be soon enough?"

"That will be fine."

We looked at each other and burst out laughing.

"The country seems open enough that I think something should be in place by the end of summer," I said.

"That seems reasonable. I will detail scouts to explore the best route, then have the surveyors with chains layout the road."

"Excellent. The first road must be leveled earth, just an improved track. Later a gravel path will be put in. Then in several years, a concrete pavement."

"Will we see a return on this investment?" He asked.

"John, I'm proud of you! You have listened to my meanderings in the evenings."

"It makes sense to consider the economics as you describe them. It is a good way to ensure you spend your money where you should."

"Economics is one consideration for certain. We also must consider critical items such as defense and the health and welfare of our people. These can trump the most economical usages."

"What's 'trump'?"

"Something that has an overriding value. The term comes from card games we used to play."

"What are card games?" He asked.

"Never mind."

"As you wish, My Lord."

Now I've done it. I've made John mad.

"John, we don't have enough paper to make decks or groups of cards so I can show you what I'm talking about. I wish we had. I would love to teach seven-card stud."

"Like when a horse is put to stud?"

Groan.

"Not really, I don't know where the term came from, but it is not from any usage here."

Thankfully the subject was dropped.

We spent time planning out a road network. Since we were on horseback, it was a general discussion.

Wendon was as distant from Saltash as any of the other local Baronies.

My goal was to have a main road from Owen-nap to Saltash. Exporting food to the London of this history was how we could earn the money to implement all my ideas.

This main road would be a two-lane highway with a level grade, good drainage, and pull-over spots. It would have a wide right of way for my first railroad.

This railroad would be like the first American railroads. A solid roadbed, but the track would be different. Like the early American tracks, the 'rail' would be a flanged piece of steel on a long wooden beam.

Any future track would have to be steel to handle the weight as cars and engines grew in size and weight. As I described this to John, he shook his head.

I didn't want to overload his thinking, so I shifted to having fresh fish delivered to our Keep.

"How could that be done?" I asked.

"The old Romans would line the sides and bottom of a cart with clay. After it hardened, they filled the cart with seawater and living fish. That way, they could sell fresh fish far inland. The trick is to have good enough roads, so the fish live through the transportation."

"That is clever, John."

So, I'm forgiven for my trumps and playing cards.

Since the Romans moved fish this way, it wasn't a new idea, so no witchcraft was involved.

"Another thing that used to be done was storing winter ice in a cave," I said.

"I have heard of that. I have never seen it done, though."

"It's lots of work, John, but a simple concept. Have you gone into a deep cave in the summertime and found it cool?"

"Yes, I have."

"So imagine in the winter we cut ice blocks out of a pond and store them in the cave. We would need sawdust between layers so they wouldn't stick together."

"Wouldn't the ice melt?" He asked.

"Yes, it would, but so slowly that some would be available for most of the summer."

"The idea of a cold drink on a hot summer day is wonderful."

"You know that ice freezes meat so that it is good for a long time?"

"I hadn't thought of that, but the wild game could be stockpiled for the lean times."

"It could, and better yet, we could raise animals for slaughter and keep the meat fresh," I said.

"We do that now. The livestock is slaughtered when we need the meat."

"But you have to feed the animal until you need the meat. This way, you can slaughter them after their growth and not have to keep feeding them."

"That is wonderful!" He exclaimed.

"People will have to become used to picking up their ice every week or so. We will have a delivery service. People will pay to drop ice off at their home or farmhouse."

"Won't the ice melt quickly?"

"Not in the iceboxes that will be sold," I said.

"What is an 'icebox'?"

"A box with two walls. Between the walls will be a layer of sawdust to act as an insulator. The ice will melt but very slowly. Every home will want one. Some of our farmers will raise cattle, other sheep. Those that raise hogs now will even have more.

Meat will be a common table item within two years."

"That will make our people healthier with a nobleman's diet."

"Yes, it will, John. Add a dairy herd for milk, chickens for meat and eggs, and our people will live well."

"People will be fleeing from the other Baronies to live here. It will end up in war," he said.

"I know. I have been debating if I should wait to be attacked or preemptively attack the Barons."

"Preemptively, that's another new word. I think it means you know they will attack you so that you will get in the first blow."

"Exactly."

"How soon will this happen?" He asked.

"Not this coming year if we do it at all."

"Good. James, back to the ice cave idea. We don't have any deep caves or caverns around here."

"We will. When one of the coal seams gives out, we will continue digging down and create our cavern. If I remember correctly, the temperature should be a constant ten degrees centigrade."

"I thought ice melts above zero degrees from your explanation."

"It does, but very slowly. The sawdust will slow down the melting. We will have at least two doors, so we have an air gap."

The explanation of the air gap took us back to the village.

"After the lumber mill, I want to build a grist mill," I said.

"Aye, they have them in the east where they grow a lot of grain. We never had enough here to justify one."

The east was generally considered the counties surrounding London. Kent, Essex, Surrey Buckinghamshire, and Hertfordshire. North was anything past those counties. Scotland was a hazy thought at most. It was known to be far away.

Wales was north of us, but since it wasn't directly connected to Cornwall, it was another world. Everywhere else was 'over there.' Over there, not being defined.

I suspect some merchants and seafarers from Saltash better understood the world.

I had drawn up a set of plans for the water portion of each mill.

The mills would be overshot vertical wheels. These were more efficient than the undershot. The undershot use water momentum to turn the wheel. The overshot wheel uses the water's weight to turn the wheel's axle, which is connected to gears to turn the sawblade or grinding stone.

We would need to site the mills near the falls where possible and then build a dam below the falls. This arrangement would give a good volume of water and create enough head pressure to keep the wheel turning.

When dumped from the buckets into the mill race, the water would feed into another collector pond which would be dammed up. This second pond would allow us to build another mill downstream of the dam.

I could see a small village growing nearby. Invariably it would be named Milltown.

I described the water layout of the site needed. John said he knew of several spots that might serve. We agreed to ride out on the morrow and check them out.

He also informed me that one of the coal seams was thinning and would soon be played out. We decided to check this out on our trip to see if it would suit as an ice cave.

It had to be near a large pond where we could cut the ice. All we needed was running water. We could divert it and build our shallow pond, which would be much safer than a naturally deep one.

Chapter 20

When we arrived in our village the Wendon headman, and his wife were assigned to one of the new brick houses for their use. The tour began at the village bathhouse and the new clothes he gave them made them look like different people.

John told me later; the wife was on our side immediately. She wanted what we had. Just looking at the villagers told her our story; they were all healthy.

After a session with the midwives, she realized her husband's life would be in jeopardy if he didn't accept all the changes. He wasn't stupid and saw how all the improvements would help his people.

It was almost too much when they were given a school tour. Common people were taught how to read, write, and understand numbers. Who had ever heard of such a thing? What use would it be?

They wouldn't have access to books or have a use for numbers.

A tour of the Monastery changed their thinking about books.

John took them back to the village, while I stayed at the Monastery. They were impressed by everything they saw. But I think the food was at the top of their list.

The monks had made tremendous progress on the printing press. It was a screw-powered, the same as squeezing apples for cider.

The breakthrough introduced molds that could be used to cast metal letters. They had all the lettering they needed to produce a page. The letters were placed in order in a box. Once the page was complete, any extra spacing was filled with blanks and the box was bound around its edges.

Once the document was completely printed, the boxes could be stored until another printing was required.

The Monks were proud of a newsletter they printed regularly. They had reinvented Poor Richards Almanac.

Being helpful, I suggested phrases. 'A stitch in time saves nine.' And 'A penny saved is a penny earned.' I didn't think Ben Franklin would mind.

The Monks were producing books by the dozens, whereas before, it would take months to produce one copy. Their best seller was a book on cleanliness. It was a combination of biblical justifications by Father Timothy and practical advice on achieving it.

Abbot Luke made ten copies of the book on how to make a microscope and shipped them to London. There was an immediate response, well immediate, for time and place. The bookseller they used wanted to know how he had produced the book and wanted as many copies as he could make.

The Abbot was planning on a run of one hundred copies. His monastery was going from poor to well-off. Soon the Bishop would show up with his hand out.

After a long discussion with the Wendon village headman and his wife, I returned to Wendon with them. Once there, we asked for a meeting with the Baron and his mother. I wanted to play this straight down the middle to show my sincere pledge to have the son the true Baron of Wendon.

I let the others do the talking. They were the ones who had to sell the Baroness. Her eight-year-old son sat in on the meeting, but you could tell he would rather be out playing.

I agreed with him about meetings, but it had to be done. The Headman and his wife made a strong case for change. Better than I could have, at least in more acceptable wording.

The Baroness had that deer in-the-headlights look, so I told her I would send a team to help implement the changes.

The first step would be to educate the other area leaders on why this should be done. Then the actual implementation. The first step was a clean water supply and waste disposal system.

Agnes would lead midwife training. She may not be able to see well, but she had become a true believer in cleanliness and was a good teacher.

I drifted back to when Agnes told me how happy she was with the changes.

"I've had to bury many babies I helped deliver. If this will save even one, it is worth it.

"You know the infant mortality rate has dropped to one in fifty births instead of two in ten?" I said.

"I do. It is a miracle you were given this knowledge."

"I don't know how I gained this knowledge, but sharing it is the Lord's work."

I may not be that religious, but I will say anything to avoid a charge of witchcraft. Before my arrival, a 'witch' had been dunked to death in a local pond. Being accused of witchcraft was a real fear.

The young Baron pulled me out of my thoughts. He was getting more restless as the meeting went on.

"Baron Wendon, would you rather be outside doing something else? I asked.

"Yes!"

"Are you current in your horsemanship and sword handling lessons?"

"Mother, Dowager Baroness, won't let me do those things," he said.

I looked over at his mother.

"His father wouldn't let him. He said he was worthless as a warrior."

"How did he know that?" I asked.

"He declared it so," she said.

"We will have lessons started; we need to identify an instructor."

Sergeant Hawkins, the man who I had left to oversee the Wendon Keep, spoke up.

"I would be glad to do that, My Lord."

I turned to the Dowager.

"Is the Sergeant acceptable?"

"Very acceptable."

I wondered about the look on her face and the reciprocal look from the Sergeant. But that was their business.

"Then please start training young Wendon here in the manly arts."

"Harrah!" yelled the young Baron.

I turned a stern look upon him.

"Young man, this depends on you doing well in your lessons. I expect you to be able to do arithmetic, spelling, reading, and writing."

That brought the young scamp down a bit.

"Yes, sir," he exaggerated.

He was going to be a handful.

"I wouldn't want to see a poor showing prevent you from having your first horse," I said.

"I will study, I promise!"

"See that you do."

With a wink to the Dowager and Sergeant, I started to depart.

"Baron Owen-nap before you leave. I have a message from my father to you."

The Dowager handed me a folded document sealed shut with wax. No fancy seals, just a plain blob of wax.

The letter contained an invitation from the Dowager's father, inviting me to visit him in Saltash. He wanted to thank me in person for how I was treating her and his grandson.

"I will tell your father I would be delighted to visit him. I'm not certain of when yet, but before winter."

"I will let him know in my next letter."

I nodded back and took my leave.

Her letters were weekly. The Dowager gave them to my people to deliver. They were brought to me, and I heated and removed the seal. Not gentlemanly conduct, but this was a conquered Barony, and it would be silly to take chances. After reading, I would reseal the letter and forward it to her father, the Ships Chandler.

Her writings were very happy with her new set of circumstances. The people were also accepting the changes.

While riding back to my Keep, I had time to think.

The look between the Dowager and the Sergeant reminded me of my needs. While I still thought of

Dory as the love of my life, that was another life ago.

As time moved on, the pain of her passing was less, but another pain grew. I was a healthy young man in need of female companionship.

There was no lack of applicants for that position. Marriage needn't be considered; having my children would be rewarding enough.

With my upbringing, I couldn't go along with that thinking. If nothing else, history has taught me the dangers of children out of wedlock and how they could be used against you.

The question was, how could I meet someone who met my criteria? A better question was, what are my criteria?

While returning to Owen-nap, I passed the turn-off to the ice cave that was in process. My original thought of using a played-out coal mine didn't work. There wasn't enough natural stone around the old coal seam to support the earth above.

Thankfully an old local knew of a small cavern. The opening was at the bottom of a shallow sinkhole. It had been the secret hideout for local lads for many a year.

The cavern was well known to all the adults in the area. They had played there in their youth. I suspect it had the pleasure of being a lovers' rendezvous over the years.

They found an opening too small for the littlest boy to crawl through at the back of the cavern. Air could be felt moving out of it, so it had to be deeper.

No one had ever tried to go further in.

They claimed a monster lived in its depths. You could hear its screams some days.

After I inspected the area, I sent a team to dig out the small opening. It turned out to be a real job. The team had to use hammers and picks to break out the rock and widen the small opening after ten feet.

At one point, it had narrowed down to a fist-sized opening. No one could have crawled back in there. It also funneled down so much that air movement through the tunnel increased its velocity. This wind moving over the rocks created the monster's scream.

To satisfy local feelings about the issue, I had Father Timothy come out and bless the opening and keep the monster at bay. The good Father kept a straight face while doing this and we didn't talk of it, but I think he knew the truth. At least, I hope he did.

Once past the narrow opening, the cavern became a large natural limestone cavern. It wasn't deep enough to keep the temperature constant, but it would be an excellent entrance to work with.

We also found a small opening at the top of the cavern where the interior airflow came from. Once we knew that, a simple exploration of the area found a series of openings, more like wide cracks that faced the prevailing wind.

The first thing we needed to do was cut a long ramp into the side of the shallow sinkhole. This ramp made it possible for horse-drawn carts to go into the cavern.

It took several weeks to cut out a passage large enough to allow a horse and cart to pass through.

Once this was done, the real work could start. The cavern would be a sheltered staging area for the ice cave entrance.

The bottom of the sinkhole was dug out another five feet without running into rock. This arrangement worked well because we filled the additional five feet with gravel and had a French drain for rainwater coming down the ramp.

I thought about how to get down another twenty feet where the temperature should be constant throughout the year. Ramps back and forth was an option but would require too much space for a reasonable slope.

I decided to dig straight down and use an elevator system. A new concern was creating airflow. With people working down there and needing to use candles or torches for light, the oxygen would be used up quickly.

We would use clay pipes and bellows to move air to the lower cavern. With no stream nearby, it would have to be hand-operated bellows. Plenty of work for the young boys.

Chapter 21

The single-lane road to Wendon was well underway and would be completed soon. The double-wide road to Saltash was a different story. We had almost reached our borders, and starting work in Saltash's area wouldn't have been polite without Baron Saltash's consent.

The road would have a wide clearing on each side so bandits couldn't set up for an ambush.

This road would be the first laid out completely by my surveying team using rods and chains. The road would be straight and have markers every kilometer. I thought in miles but was trying to institute the metric system, so I bit the bullet and made it happen.

Another change I noticed over time was the language translation going on in my head. At first, I knew it was happening. I would hear in the original Cornish, but my mind would translate it to English and vice versa.

Now it happened without any noticeable translation. It was like I had learned the language and now thought in it.

As the surveying teams laid out the road and markers, I had my maps updated by the Monks to reflect greater accuracy. I intended to have all lands under my control mapped like a US Geographical Survey. Well, more like they would have done it in about 1850.

It would take many years to develop and launch a GPS satellite.

It was time I made a trip to Saltash. I had to establish relations with the Baron. Hopefully, they will be good relations.

This trip wouldn't be as simple as others I had made. I needed to take a small entourage to establish that I was a serious Baron.

I sent a rider to Saltash, letting John Chandler, the father of the Dowager Baroness of Wendon, know I was responding to his invitation. The rider would then let the Baron of Saltash know I was coming and request an audience upon arrival.

Upon the rider's return with acceptance by both the Chandler and Baron, I was ready to visit Saltash. John Steward would be in charge of Owen-nap until I returned.

My travel party seemed large, but John Steward told me that any less would be foolish. I needed guards from bandits and others to show my importance.

I wouldn't argue the point, he knew better than me. I did decide that something had to be done about these bandits that everyone talked of though. They weren't Robin Hood and his band of merry men. Cutthroat killers are more like it.

There were four men-at-arms with swords and four crossbowmen. Linda, the small girl I had assigned as my runner. Father Timothy to show that I was a good Christian. Two Monks to demonstrate Mathematics, one Monk to sell their latest books.

Two Midwives to talk about and teach cleanliness in the birthing process if allowed. And finally, a man to act as my body servant.

There were also animals loaded with tents, food, products for sale, and gifts.

On the trip there, I was glad that I had introduced stirrups locally. I'm certain they were in use elsewhere, but not here. It would make riding easier and save my poor backside.

It was a four-day trip of forty miles. The first night we covered fifteen miles and camped at our border. This travel was on the good road that I had built. Things would slow down the rest of the way.

My new road stopped abruptly at the border. There was a five-foot-tall marker with Owen-nap chiseled into the side facing Saltash. It also stated 24 Kilometers to Owen-nap Keep with markers each kilometer along the way.

On the side facing Owen-nap, Saltash had been chiseled in. There was a blank left for the number of kilometers. We wouldn't be able to survey the road until Baron Saltash allowed it.

I was surprised to learn that Chaucer was right in reporting that travelers told stories to help the trip along. The second night I had to tell a tale. So I told the Miller's tale from the Canterbury Tales to my fellow travelers' great mirth and merriment.

Is it plagiarism when you tell a story before it is written?

Half a day before we arrived at Saltash, we were met by a party of five men-at-arms from the Baron. I was told they were here to guide us safely into Saltash. Bandits, you know.

I thanked them and invited their leader to ride with me. As we rode along, it became obvious that he had the same goal as me. Me to learn about Saltash, his to learn about me.

The Sergeant was a better interrogator than me because I talked more than him, but I was very careful about revealing my true story. It appeared well known that I had fallen from a horse, laid unconscious for days, and woken up with new knowledge.

"Sergeant, I have no idea how I gained that knowledge. It was there when I woke."

"Did you have any visitations while you were asleep?" He asked.

"None. I don't remember being thrown from the horse. The last thing I remember is getting ready to go to the stables. The next thing I knew, I was waking up in my bed with a terrible headache."

"Very strange, My Lord. You must have been God-touched while asleep."

"It seems so, but I can't vouch for it."

"That is usually the case with true God-touched. Charlatans claim visions and great portents."

It was good to know that I had taken the right approach.

"Baron Saltash will be interested in your new knowledge. He is always trying to make things better in our land," the Sergeant said.

I did get a better description of the Barony of Saltash. It centered around the port of Saltash and was a prosperous town of over a thousand souls. There were two other small villages in the Barony.

The villages were about ten miles or sixteen kilometers east and west of Saltash, almost to the border of the adjoining Baronies. Saltash was at a long-standing peace with these Baronies.

I would think so. Saltash controlled the only port for many miles along the coastline.

The Baron himself was old, over sixty years! Almost ancient. Few lived much longer in that day and age. He had several children by his wives, both deceased. The only surviving child was a daughter of twenty-two years.

According to the Sergeant, she ran the Keep for her father, acting as his Steward. Well educated, she ran the Keep with an iron hand. I tried to picture her from the Sergeant's description. She was tall for a woman, with blonde hair, blue eyes, a full figure, and fair of face.

I realized that she was being built up as a future wife. More likely, she was as ugly as a fence post and had a screeching voice from bossing people around. I couldn't decide if the full figure translated into fat as a hog and I wasn't about to ask. Time would tell.

When we arrived at Saltash, my first impression was good. It was a walled city with guards at its gate. The walls were true fortifications. It went a long way in explaining the peace between the Baronies.

The other Barons couldn't successfully attack Saltash; if he didn't attack them, there was peace. I asked and was told the Baron had the walls erected early in his reign, almost forty years ago.

The streets were wide and clean, and the people were healthy looking and well-dressed. They seemed cheerful and didn't reflect resentment at their lot in life.

The people's looks spoke well of the Baron's governing.

The Baron's Keep was more in the manner of a Norman Keep. No wonder no one attacked him. I bet his men-at-arms were numerous and well-trained. Peace through strength would be his motto. Not that it would be put that way, but that was the result.

Arriving at the Keep, I was taken to a small suite of rooms to freshen up. It had a sitting room, bedroom, and, as my nose told me, a garderobe.

The garderobe was one area where my new knowledge was desperately needed.

I would let the Midwives explain why it was necessary to keep them clean and how to do it.

After freshening up, I was taken to an audience with Baron Saltash. He was waiting in a small room with a table and real chairs.

The Baron was a tall man starting to stoop with age. The years had given him a worn look, but strong at the same time. The Baron was a man out and about, living an active life, not someone hiding behind his walls.

He met me halfway into the room, clasping arms at the wrist as common between equals. If this weren't all show, I would have no problems working with the Baron.

He introduced me to his daughter Eleanor who stood beside him.

I was wrong in my guesses. Eleanor's voice was melodious. She was slender with well-proportioned hips and breasts. As to the Sergeant's statement of her fair face he was wrong. She is beautiful, movie star beautiful. I restrained myself from asking her to turn around. She must look like a vision from the back.

Dory always called me an ass-man or, at times, an ass.

I managed to croak out that I was pleased to meet her. The smile on her face said she was used to this reaction from men.

We sat at the table, and wine was offered. It was better than any I had tasted since awakening. Not great, but not bad.

"Is this a Pinot Noir from Burgundy?" I asked.

From the look on his face, I had just stepped in it.

"Yes, it is, My Lord."

"Please call me James, or we will be My Lording it all day."

"You can call me William."

"You can call me Lady Eleanor" Eleanor said.

I was told that I had to earn the right to call her by name.

"Certainly, My Lady."

Baron Saltash, or William as I would call him in private, followed up on my comment on the Pinot Noir.

"This wine is new to us this week. May I ask how you know of it?"

Uh oh. I had to think quickly.

"I don't know, William. It just came to me like many other things since I woke from being thrown from a horse."

He wasn't comfortable with that answer, but it was all I could give. There was no way I could tell him that Dory and I occasionally enjoyed a glass of red wine with our dinner. Not often, as I still was afraid of my family's alcoholism.

"I have heard that you were God-touched. It is hard to believe, but what I have heard confirms that," William said.

"I don't claim to be God-touched. If God touched me, it would be to smite me for my former behavior."

"That is another thing. You have changed your attitude towards everything since awakening. Before, you took after your father, an entitled noble brat with no care for his people. Now all I hear is praise for how you care for them."

"I'm not that good of a man. I have realized that a strong, healthy population is the true wealth of my Barony. From what I have seen so far, you believe the same."

"My father taught me my beliefs, sometimes with a stick. You have changed with no guidance."

"I can't explain it. It just is."

As I spoke, I kept looking between her and her father. I wanted her approval. Who was I kidding? I wanted her!

Chapter 22

As Eleanor spoke, I realized she was beautiful, had poise, and was well-spoken. All that said, I didn't know her. She might be a shrew for all I knew. While it might be fun to tame a shrew, would it be worth the effort?

Besides all the wonderful attributes standing before me, I needed an intelligent partner. Would she be the one? Time would tell, and I was eager to find out.

Eleanor continued, "My Lord, you certainly have been the talk of our court."

"All good, I hope."

"Not good or bad, all are wondering where you are headed with the changes you have instituted in your Barony. There is some fear, especially with how easily you defeated Baron Wendon."

"I hope my actions after the small fight reduced some of that fear," I said.

"Puzzled is more like it."

While this conversation was going on the Baron sat listening intently. I was in a good cop, bad cop situation.

This thought was confirmed when the Baron spoke, "This is why we are reluctant to deal with you. Too many unknowns. What are your intentions for your Barony?"

"To better the lives of everyone in my Barony. Strength lies in the people, not your number of armsmen. I believe in quality over quantity."

Eleanor burst out, "You have read Seneca?"

I had, in another lifetime.

"The Monks have a good library."

Now I had to make certain that Seneca was one of the manuscripts they had.

"Where did you learn Latin?" She asked?

"From the Monks."

Another famous line came to mind, 'Oh, what a tangled web we weave….' I had to come clean with her soon or get the Monks to back my story.

Here I came to establish trade relations. Instead, I was caught up in my own story.

Turning to the Baron, "I hope you will allow me to trade directly with the merchants here in Saltash."

The Baron replied, "Like you, I want the best for my people for the same reasons you speak of. Yes, you, like all others, have permission to trade."

"My Lord, you seem to know what is happening in my Barony. Are you aware of the roads we are building?" I asked.

"Of course, we are watching with great interest. You are expending large sums of money to what end?"

"To make trade easier."

"You will have to trade a lot to recoup your investment."

These weren't the words he used. They were the words my mind interpreted them as.

"You are correct."

I explained to him and Eleanor what I had accomplished so far. We now have a calorie surplus with new farming tools and crop rotation methods. These changes would enable us to ship grain to market.

The Baron chuckled as he told me how impressed he was with my buying the grain being moved through my Barony. It might upset him, but he thought it was a shrewd move. All the costs would be passed on to the merchants in London.

He expressed concern that it would eventually lead to war with the Barons surrounding me.

I shrugged. This bit of body language seemed to be universal.

I told them of the Monk's printing press, making books generally available. This invention enabled me to open schools for all in my land.

The way the Baron looked at me, I could tell he thought the Monks had little to do with the invention. It was my story, and I was sticking to it.

From there, I explained my views on cleanliness. I offered to demonstrate this with one of the microscopes I brought.

Eleanor almost danced as she said, "So it is true you have reduced the infant death rate?"

"Yes."

"Will you share what needs to be done?"

"Our most senior and best midwife has accompanied me and is eager to share what she has learned."

All this led to a conversation about keeping the village and Keep clean. Ensuring the drinking water was clean, moving the middens out of the village, nightsoil collection, baths, and laundries.

My meeting had started early in the day. We talked about my changes until the midafternoon meal. They continued until supper time.

I thought my visit to Saltash would be three days, but now it looked like it would be a week.

The Baron gave his steward orders to gather all the midwives in the Barony for a lecture and to demonstrate why some changes had to be made.

It would be held in two days in the Keep's main hall. His Keep, unlike mine, was a fortified structure with many rooms. In truth, it could be called a small castle.

The Baron agreed that I would spend the next day with John Chandler, the father of the Dowager Baroness of Wendon. This visit would be all about trade.

The Baron told me again that he was William, not My Lord.

I took a leaf from John Steward's book and replied, "Yes, Lord William."

I thought the old guy would choke. He laughed so hard.

The next morning, I kept my appointment with John Chandler. I was well-received as the savior of his daughter and grandson.

Over coffee, he asked for the details of my battle with the previous Baron and my rationale for letting his descendants live. I told him I would share the entire story if he would tell me how to have a constant supply of coffee.

"There is a merchant in London who imports it from Turkey. I first tasted it on a visit to London. I'm surprised you know of this drink. Most people think it too bitter when they first taste it," he said.

How do I answer that?

"A peddler had some for sale. I tried it. You are right; it was very bitter, but I found it to wake me up and to be more alert."

He accepted that answer. Peddlers were a strange breed and came up with all sorts of things. Not to be dependable for a regular supply of anything, but always having something you seemed to need.

I related the entire tale, including my reasoning for allowing the young Baron and his mother to live. You could see him relax as I finished. My decision was based on reason, not emotion.

We talked of my buying the grain on its way to Saltash. I expressed my concern that the grain merchants might take exception to my action.

"The grain merchants all admire you. They passed the price increases on to London with an additional ten percent. They blamed this all on you. I wouldn't visit London soon if I were you," he said.

"I don't need to go to London now, so it is moot. What I need are products sent to London for sale."

At that, Chandler's ears perked up.

"What do you want to send?"

I had arranged for the products I brought to be delivered here. I first showed the improved plow.

"If this gives you such a farming advantage, why share?" He asked.

"Because I don't like to think of people starving."

I didn't mention the better crop rotation. One has to have some secrets, after all.

"You can sell the first shipments, but the Blacksmiths of London will soon be competing with you. The price of shipping will put you out of the market," he said.

"Maybe the first year. I didn't tell you that this is a better grade of steel, and theirs will fail quickly while an Owen-nap plow will last for years."

I showed him the Owen-nap mark on the plow. I had settled for a standing Griffon similar to the one used in Poland in my old time.

Below the Griffon was a serial number. I explained that every plow would have a unique number. I taught him how to read the number with the date of manufacture and order of manufacture.

"Why would you do that?" He asked.

"If there are reports of failure of the plows, we can compare the numbers and see if there is a pattern of failure, like a bad lot of steel."

"How can you tell if it is a bad lot?"

"We keep a record of the lot used for each plow and a sample of all steel lots. This numbering is called traceability."

"Anyone can make your mark and put a number on a plow."

"They don't know that the marks are low radius marks."

I showed him how the marks had a gentle curve rather than the sharp edge of the normal stamp.

"A simple finger running over the surface will tell if it is ours. I know the counterfeiters will catch on after a while, but that is true of all manufactured items."

He agreed to ship the first lot of ten plows to London to see if they would sell. We both agreed that a demonstration of the plows in a field would show their worth.

One of my single farmers agreed to accompany the plows for the demonstration. I doubted he would return. Once they have seen gay Paree, how can you get them back down on the farm?

"We have started to build the pottery works and will soon be able to ship pots to London. I also have ten spinning wheels that are foot powered for sale. These wheels will outperform the standard spinning wheel by almost doubling the production. They are faster, and the worker doesn't tire as easily," I said.

After several more cups of coffee, oh, how I had missed it, we agreed on asking prices for the plow and spinning wheel with his commission built in.

Lastly, I brought out a microscope setup. After a demonstration using a hair from my head, he was eager to sell them. I had a price of ten silver in mind. He told me they should fetch one hundred silver!

When I explained how you could see little animals that poisoned us, he thought they might be worth five hundred silver. I told him not to get greedy.

He backed down on raising the price again, but it was more to keep in my good graces rather than not being greedy.

He accompanied me to my horse in his stable when I was about to leave and saw the stirrups added to my saddle before the trip. I hadn't intended to show the stirrups at this time.

These were a simple add-on to my English-style saddle. I had a Western-style saddle being made, but it would be many months before Tanner would have the materials ready.

John Chandler was no dummy. He saw the stirrups utility at once. Why they weren't in common use, he didn't understand. I explained that in some parts of the world, they were.

"I suppose that peddler who had coffee had these?"

His tone of voice said he didn't believe me. Well, I had been lying.

"Yes, Sir, it was him who had these."

He snorted but said no more. I invited him to the midwife demonstration of the microscope and lecture on cleanliness on the morrow. He gladly accepted.

As a last comment, he told me he would send money to his daughter and grandson to help support the Barony. He had refused to do it while that drunk was alive. If he had known then what he knew now, he would never have given his daughter's hand in marriage to that bum.

Later I was invited to dine privately with the Baron and Eleanor. I was all for this. The more time I got to spend with Eleanor, the better. I wanted to get to know her.

I was mesmerized by the young lady; I hardly knew what I was eating. She had it all, at least on the surface. I wanted to get below the surface of her personality, and also her clothes.

Chapter 23

While my new young body was responding to Eleanor in every way possible, I made a point of being polite during dinner. I didn't want to offend her or scare her away. Besides, her dad was present.

Dinner was a leisurely affair where we discussed how we would like to develop our respective Baronies. Baron Saltash and Eleanor were enthusiastic about expanding trade. With the largest seaport in Cornwall, it made sense.

My plans were centered around food production and the manufacturing of trade goods. Our plans meshed. Without committing, we talked about how we could help each other.

Our crops this fall were a resounding success. He was astonished when I told the Baron how much I wished to send to London. That wasn't even counting any that the other Barons would want to sell.

He told me that John Chandler was the man to work with. He was ethical and made things happen.

I shared what he wanted to charge for a microscope, and the Baron didn't understand why I wouldn't charge the higher price. Eleanor took my side that the people who needed help wouldn't get it if they were too expensive.

We argued back and forth for a while, with Eleanor getting more excited in making her case that I was correct.

We finally agreed to disagree with the Baron. As I took my leave, the Baron looked very satisfied. It made me wonder if Eleanor and I had been played.

Was the Baron trying to push us together?

The next day I met the real Eleanor.

She was at the meeting with the midwives. Several of them rushed over to hug her when she entered the room.

I was standing with John Chandler at the time. I commented that they all seemed to know her.

"She has been helping them for over five years. They consider her an apprentice in training. She is known for tearing into husbands who don't treat their wives properly."

Baron Saltash introduced me. In turn, I introduced Father Timothy and Senior Midwife Agnes. Agnes blushed when I called her Senior Midwife as it was news. I paused with a surprised look.

"Agnes, didn't we tell you all our other midwives voted you to be senior over them? They asked me to give you this."

I handed her a new armband. It was the same as the one she wore, except a laurel wreath surrounded the red cross. I led the applause for her.

Father Timothy was the first speaker. He made the biblical case that cleanliness is next to godliness. This talk was well received as the midwives present were already clean by our original standards.

When he was finished, I shared the story about collecting nightsoil and moving the hogs out of our village. When I got to the woman, who was now known as poopy breath, the room erupted in laughter. We lived in a bawdy day and age.

The Baron was slapping his knee, and Eleanor was holding a handkerchief to her mouth.

Then came the serious demonstration. Agnes had become a pro at showing how bacteria lived everywhere but could be killed by boiling water.

She even had a booklet to hand out describing everything that needed to be done for sterile clean childbirth. There were pictures made from hand-cut blocks for those who couldn't read.

She gave them out for free at the course, but the Monks had printed several hundred to send to London for sale. They kept the price down to one silver so everyone could afford them.

I smiled at the first page, which told where the booklet originated. The Owen-nap Monastery Press Cornwall printed it. It had authors Agnes, Senior Midwife of Owen-nap with Father Timothy of Owen-nap, and Editor as Abbot Luke. It was under the imprimatur of Baron Owen-nap.

I love it. It is the start of my Barony being considered a seat of learning. The important part is that my people took my base ideas and expanded on them.

I made a mental note to have a farming book printed describing four field rotations. This booklet would reduce grain sales profits in the long run but would lead to a healthier country. Not that England was a country yet. At best, it could be called a group of former Roman provinces hunting for a new home.

Agnes's lecture went well. Many questions were asked and answered. They were good questions.

There didn't seem to be any resistance to the new ideas.

Actually, I think Agnes was confirming things that had been suspected all along.

Eleanor participated in the session with knowledgeable questions. While not the leader of the Saltash midwives, she was treated with respect, more from her knowledge than her title.

I liked this girl. Not that I was in a hurry to do anything about it. I had to get to know her better, but she was the first woman I had met here that I was interested in. I had no idea if she was interested in me.

Since I had heard Agnes's presentation several times and had given the first one, I allowed my mind to wander.

I had scouts traveling to the other Baronies, picking up information. There was a need for a more formal system. Having people passing through occasionally was one thing. Having embedded agents was another.

John Steward and I were stretched thin these days with all we had going on. I needed to identify someone to be my spymaster. The person had to have strong connections with Owen-nap. The old or to-be-new CIA in the United States learned to recruit from the British.

They would have a recruiter at universities like Yale and Harvard. The recruiter would identify a candidate with long and strong roots in the county.

We didn't have a university to select from, but we did know which families had strong ties to the Barony. John would identify candidates, and we would interview them separately. They had to have some education but, more importantly, a streak of cruelty to do whatever it took to get the job done.

They wouldn't be publicly employed. But would be given an innocuous title such as Keeper of Records.

They would recruit men and women to take jobs in each Barony. We would use the cell system so no agent's capture would bring the network down.

Ideally, they would be employed at an Inn or Taphouse where the local officials and men at arms hung out. One of their goals would be to recruit an agent that would work inside the Keep.

I would have to develop a course on spy craft, including the fine arts of blackmail, bribery, and threats. It was a dirty business, but I needed to know what the other Barons were up to.

There would have to be a communication system for regular reports and an emergency method when things went bad.

Then I realized I didn't know if any of the Baronies had an Inn or Taphouse. There weren't either in Owen-nap.

If we were going to expand trade, we would need both. I had to look into that when I got home.

Home? Now that was a change in thinking.

Clapping at the end of the lecture brought me back as Agnes presented red cross armbands to all present. The only ones who didn't immediately put theirs on were the Baron and me.

Afterward, I complimented Eleanor on her involvement. Her blush was the first girlish emotion she had shown me. That and a lowering of her eyes as she thanked me.

Maybe she was a little interested in me.

Again, too soon. There will be many more trips to Saltash. I even extended an invitation to the Baron and her to visit Owen-nap to see firsthand what we were accomplishing. They both responded positively.

It would have to be in the Winter when things slowed down everywhere. Travel conditions permitting.

I had to get home and ensure my Keep was ready to receive them.

I spent another day with John Chandler working out the details of our first trading shipments. The grain could be sold at once. The plows, microscopes, and spinning wheels need more groundwork in London to sell them.

That meant I had to return to Owen-nap and come up with sales representatives to send along with the products. Chandler volunteered to send two experienced merchants to help set up a shop and get things started.

He even told me what guilds had to be bribed and what officials paid off to do business in London. It seemed like organized crime until I realized it was the beginning of a legal taxation system.

When you got down to it, all governments were protection rackets. When held in check, it worked well. The system would collapse, usually through a revolution, when the corruption grew too bad.

While at Chandler's, I told him I wanted to start several cattle herds. One for beef and another for dairy. I was hoping he knew where I could buy cattle to start the herds.

He knew of a few individuals who kept cows. They were in lots of two or three. I would have to send a buyer out to the farms in the area to see what was for sale.

We discussed what would be a fair price. In each case, we would need as many cows as possible. And at least two bulls for redundancy and to minimize inbreeding.

Then there was a place to accumulate the purchased cattle and the problem of herding them to Owen-nap once the herds had been gathered.

Chandler offered the use of one of his farms as a gathering point. But I would have to provide the purchasing agents and drivers.

All this led to a discussion about the ice cave I had built and how it would preserve meat until needed. John was impressed when I explained that ice boxes and insulated containers would be offered for sale and an ice delivery service would be set up.

It would take at least two years before my beef herd would be large enough to start harvesting the animals. John thought the beef herd would work well for me but questioned the wisdom of a dairy herd.

Milk spoils quickly. Collecting it in large quantities would be a waste of time and effort.

I explained how refrigeration using an ice box would extend milk's shelf life. The term shelf life was new, but he immediately understood the concept.

I proceeded to tell him about pasteurization. I even gave credit to Louis Pasteur. John told me he wanted to meet the gentleman and asked if it would be possible to arrange it.

Thinking quickly, I told him it wasn't possible as Pasteur had died. How could I explain that he lived hundreds of years in the future and now may never be born?

His next argument was that the dairy business wouldn't be profitable. I countered that I was more interested in the health of my people. He accepted that argument.

I won him to my side when I asked him if he knew how cheese was made. He opened his eyes at that.

"Now that can be profitable, and cheese keeps," he said.

"Think of what we could do if we put cheese on ice in a ship's hold and sent it to London."

"Now, that would be money!"

I was calling it London in my words, but it was coming through to John as Londonium. I had tried to figure out how this was happening, but all I got was a headache from my efforts.

It was time to head back to Owen-nap. My tasks here were completed. Before I left, Baron Saltash asked for one last meeting.

We met in private. Eleanor, who was usually at these meetings, was elsewhere. I soon understood why.

"Owen-nap, you must be aware of my situation. I'm getting old and do not have much time left. I must look to the future of my people and my daughter Eleanor."

I didn't reply but nodded my head in understanding.

The Baron continued, "Eleanor is capable of running this Barony, but we both know the other Barons would be on her like a pack of wolves. They would either force her into marriage or take Saltash by force, killing her."

I now saw where he was going with this and, after what I had seen of the young lady, had no objection. I needed a wife, helpmeet, confidant, stand-in, mother to my children, and most of all, a friend. She could be all of these.

Chapter 24

Now that the harvest was in and the first snow had fallen, it was time for school to restart. The first day was a circus. All but one student had shown up. The absentee had broken his leg the previous day. His parents sent word he would be there the next week.

We had set up four tents for registration. There were two hundred and forty-five students in this winter's class.

Students were assigned tents alphabetically by their last names. From the groans of the teacher Monks making certain each was in the correct line, there was much remedial work to be done, just like after my summer breaks.

Other tents were set up to distribute class materials such as wax writing boards and styli.

There was another set of tents for males and females to have a physical inspection by the midwives. The public reason was to look for disease. The actual reason for signs of abuse. We were lucky this year with none evident.

In the past, men or some women would be extremely abusive to their families. I had made it known that physical abuse wouldn't be tolerated. It must have been a strong message because two men left the Barony. Another stayed, and I had him hanged when he kept it up.

Mental abuse was an area that we were weak in. I had never read any books on it, so I had no references to work with.

The midwives had issued themselves a new armband that identified a nurse, one who could help with all illnesses. The first books I wrote were short ones on various illnesses and how the human body worked with some illustrations.

My memory is a wonderful thing. These books were elementary but were the beginnings of the medical profession here and now.

Besides the official school tents were local entrepreneurs selling armbands proclaiming one to specialize in reading, writing, or arithmetic.

There were even shirts with my coat of arms marking the start of the t-shirt industry. They were roughly handstitched on the back of a flax vest, but the idea was there.

I don't know how word had spread, but there was a juggler, a puppet show, and tumblers. There were stands selling refreshments.

The first day of school was a circus. I loved it.

Classes would continue until it was time for spring planting. I heard one mother tell another that it was a blessing the children had something to do all winter rather than be underfoot.

Since it was a grand occasion, I had to make a speech. I kept it short, welcoming the old and new students. I told the audience I hoped the students would devise a play for the Christmas season and put it on for all to attend.

Father Timothy immediately cornered me and asked how I would make certain it was reverent to the season.

"As the play director, I'm certain you will make that happen."

Talk about conflicting emotions! He looked elated about being in charge while asking himself, "Why me, Lord?"

The Lord he was asking wasn't me.

The first day of school was a complete victory, in my estimation. While the school year was shorter than those in my original time period, I was confident they would learn as much. These were willing students.

And if they weren't willing, the Monks would teach to the tune of that proverbial hickory stick.

Of course, our sticks were beech, as hickory was found in North America. Still, I liked the song.

The first lumber mill was in full operation. While it was turning out a good number of finished boards, it was nothing like what we would need soon.

I was thrilled when two men from the village approached me about starting a lumber mill using waterpower. One of them had seen an operation like that in Germania when serving with a Roman Legion.

They had identified a site along one of the rivers that would suit their purpose. Lots of running water and plenty of trees upstream. They even had a business plan. Granted, it was rudimentary, but it was a plan.

They had considered the cost of building a mill, including the huge cost of saw blades, a fee for cutting my trees, and payroll. The only problem was they didn't know how much finished boards would sell for.

I was so enthusiastic that I told them I would pay them cost plus ten percent for the first two years. They took me up on my offer, but later John told me they would try to sell elsewhere for much more.

I didn't care as they now had a safety net, and one thing not in their business plan was Barony taxes. The more they made, the more the Barony coffers made.

The new lumber mill wouldn't be in operation until early summer, so the only boards that would be available would be from the manual sawmill.

The manual mill wouldn't cut it even in the short run. No pun intended. I needed a lot of boards to finish the interior of the newly rebuilt Keep. And I wanted to get iceboxes going as soon as possible.

I calculated that we needed four manual sawmills running along with logging crews to keep them fed. I talked to John about it, and he informed me that since it was winter, plenty of farmers and their sons would sign up for the work.

One of my goals was to have iceboxes available this summer. We would need plenty of lumber for that project. There would be a lot of trees cut, and land cleared, which could be converted to farmland.

In my future, the great forests of Europe had been denuded for firewood and construction materials. With my introduction of coal and Franklin-type stoves, this would be avoided. Oops, had to invent that stove. No matter what, I would strive to keep parkland available.

With the first heavy freezing of our manmade pond, our icehouse operation was underway, and the ice cave had been dug out completely.

I had planned on using a bellows system to provide fresh air down to the lower cavern where the ice was stored. Instead, the Supervisor came to me with a better idea.

They would keep a coal fire burning in the ice cavern, drawing fresh air into it. I had forgotten this was known technology for just about forever. It had been in use for over four thousand years.

Not as much work for small boys, but we were always short of workers.

In the meantime, ice was being cut into blocks at the ponds and stored underground in the new cavern. Twenty-five and fifty-pound blocks were being cut.

I imagined that when ice boxes were in general use, people would put up a sign to indicate to the iceman what size block they wanted to be delivered. In my youth, it was a red sign for twenty-five pounds and blue for fifty.

Another project that I had underway but would take until summer to complete was building an Inn.

Thankfully the taphouse proved a lot easier.

I told our brewer what I wanted. The next thing I knew, a new pavilion was erected near those at the well. Three sides were closed off with an inside wall to create a storeroom. A bar, table, chairs, and instant tavern. Of course, anyone walking by could see who was drinking and their condition.

Several men complained, but many more wives stated it was just fine. I kept out of it.

While the Keep was rebuilt, I stayed in an unoccupied long house. Several rooms were divided out by curtains and all my furnishings were brought over. There was plenty of room left over, so I had some additional bedrooms curtained off.

The rest of the people who lived in the keep had either moved into one of the new brick houses or slept in one of the other empty longhouses. That longhouse also acted as the common room and dining hall for all the Keep residents.

A temporary kitchen had been built between the longhouses. This separation was needed because of fire danger. The refurbished Keep would have improved ovens out of wrought iron instead, making the kitchen much safer.

The next day a rider informed me that Baron Saltash and his daughter were on their way for a visit and would arrive on the morrow.

My first thought was to panic. How would I clean the place up to look presentable? I then stopped and realized that I was channeling my long-dead mother. The quick straightening up of the house was her first reaction to any surprise company.

Her reaction was to straighten the house, mine to straighten the Barony. I sent her a silent apology for the thoughts I used to have.

Instead of cleaning the house, I asked John to ensure that the guest rooms in my longhouse were ready for them. Then I took a walk around the village to see its condition.

I went through it every day, but after a while, you don't see things anymore. I was looking with a critical eye now and was pleased with what I saw.

What used to be about fifty hovels, was now a village of over two hundred brick houses with eight hundred residents. The streets were clean, and there were no obnoxious odors. Most importantly, there was a robust working population going about their day.

Not everyone was cheerful, but the dourest was well fed and clothed. You can't make everyone happy.

I wondered how I should greet Eleanor. I had an understanding with her father that we were to wed but hadn't talked to her. Things were certainly different in the here and now.

It would be best to have a private conversation with her as soon as possible. That is, if she didn't try to kill me outright.

I met them at the entrance to the village. The walls around the village weren't complete yet but the gatehouse was in place. Maybe I was thinking too big, but I had them building it for a town of ten thousand rather than eight hundred.

After profuse greetings, I asked John Steward to show the Baron his rooms. I would take Eleanor to hers. Clumsy, I know, but I had to talk to her alone. This situation may be normal to her, but I had serious culture shock.

Once alone, "Lady Eleanor, has your father spoken to you of what he desires?"

"You mean our marriage? You aren't trying to back out, are you?"

"No. No, but I want to ensure that it meets your approval."

Now she looked puzzled.

"Why should I approve? My father's duty is to find the best husband for our Barony and me. I think he has done that."

Inside I felt relief. Outside I went to my knee. I knew this part well.

"Lady Eleanor of Saltash, will you do me the honor of being my wife?"

Evidently, Lady Eleanor didn't know her part from her confused look, but she recovered quickly.

She replied, "I would be honored to be your wife."

I had inherited my down time mother's jewelry. There was a beautiful gold ring with a sapphire inset. It was her wedding ring. Both my parents died when I was an infant, so I never knew or thought of them. The I as in the Baron whose body I was inhabiting.

I placed the ring on her bare left ring finger. Being bare made me wonder why. She had rings on most of her fingers. She must have anticipated this. I had dodged a bullet.

I took a chance and put my arms around her. She came eagerly, and it was more her kissing me first than me kissing her and it wasn't an innocent kiss. Dory and I had a wonderful marriage and good sex. I could see this was going to be a different level. I hoped I could keep up!

Chapter 25

Eleanor's father's return interrupted our kissing. She promptly proved that some things never change. She immediately ran to him with her finger held upright so he could see the engagement ring.

A huge smile lit up his face. He grabbed his daughter in a huge hug and swung her around. He finally let her go and came to me.

I backed up slightly, not wanting the same hug. The old Baron held out his hand, and we took each other's wrists.

"Congratulations, my boy, or should I say, Son?"

From his looks, the fate of his daughter and Barony had weighed on him for a long time. The relief on his face was evident.

"Whatever you want, My Lord Baron Dad."

That got another laugh out of him.

"As you can tell from my excitement, this is good for my daughter and me. While my health remains good, I'm getting old, and we both have been concerned about the fate of Saltash. None of the other Barons surrounding us would have been good husbands for Eleanor or Barons for Saltash."

While talking, a female servant came into the room to straighten things out. While Eleanor didn't speak to her, she waved her hand as all newly engaged do. The servant smiled at Eleanor and nodded her head.

I couldn't stand it, "Marian, you may tell all that Eleanor consented to be my bride."

That was like a dam broke. Marian rushed over to admire the ring. She and Eleanor retreated to the other side of the room to discuss the gory details of its presentation. I hadn't any doubt the whole Barony would know by nightfall.

John Steward walked into the room about that time. I couldn't figure out how he knew, but the man who had been like a father to me had a large smile and his congratulations ready.

William, John, and I started to plan the wedding. They took the lead in the conversation. I felt a little nervous about this conversation. How dare we, mere men, plan a wedding.

I was correct in my feelings. Once Eleanor, Marian, and Eleanor's maid heard our conversation, they let us know in no uncertain terms this was women's work. I wisely kept my mouth shut when criticized by one of my servants.

Eleanor informed me that I would accompany her after our noonday meal to see the local priest to have the banns posted. After that, my next chore would be to show up for the wedding. I suspect the Caveman had the same instructions.

We, men, did the logical thing and retreated. The ladies remained behind to discuss more important matters. As we exited the longhouse, more women came in. How did they know?

Everyone but me seemed to have some line of communication that kept them current to the minute.

John and I gave William a walking tour of the village. He was amazed at all we had accomplished in a relatively short time.

"William, it is all due to having a calorie surplus," I said.

He had never heard this term before but got its meaning immediately.

"So you have healthy people to accomplish more?"

"That and our improved farming methods take fewer people to farm the land. To avoid starvation and to have the extra food, we have people coming from other Baronies."

"Even with the extra labor, what I see here is impressive. All of this results from your falling off of a horse?"

I don't think he believed that story for a minute.

"Yes, My Lord."

My answer told him that was my story and that I was sticking to it. Maybe one day I could tell him the truth, but not today.

The new Keep walls got his attention.

"How did you erect these so fast? Of course, I recognize the concrete, but how did you get it to stay in place?" He asked.

I explained the use of forms and rebar, which led to a discussion of how I had so much iron available. The next thing you know, we were on horseback to our new factory, the ironworks.

Tom Smith's, the village blacksmith's operations had grown so large he had to set up a second facility. The ironworks were out by the iron ore seams, which now also had a smelter.

The blacksmith was more of a manager than a smith anymore. His lead apprentice, who had almost completed his apprenticeship, was now in charge of the village smithy. His second in command was in charge of daily operations at the ironworks.

Tom rotated back and forth between the two and took care of the business side of things. He was becoming a wealthy man.

The ironworks had a different setup than the smithy. The smithy still worked on traditional lines where each worker completed the project.

At the ironworks, we had set up an elementary production line. I say we because Tom and I had developed the plan over several mugs of beer as I led him to new ideas.

After he fed them back to me, I praised his forward thinking and approved his plan. I even provided the initial investment as a silent partner. It turned out that the concept of a silent partner was well-known.

The ironworks were currently producing rebar and crossbow parts. The rebar was easy as the molten wrought iron was poured into long clay tubes. When the iron had cooled, the clay was broken away, and we had a ten-foot length of rebar.

The rebar would then be reheated on a large bed of coals and heat welded by our pony-powered hammer.

The long-term goal was a water-powered hammer. But that would take rerouting a stream and creating a pond with a dam to provide enough flow to turn the wheel. I was proud of Tom and his crew for coming up with this without my input.

The crossbow parts had many more operations, as each component had several steps. It took my invention of gauge blocks and a caliper with a fine thread screw to achieve the true interchangeability of parts.

Our first efforts had been by brute force. Now they were coming out the same after each operation. Tom had twenty employees working on the different steps. Each person was responsible for a specific step.

Tom was rigid with his employees, working on only one process step. It would take more counseling over several mugs of beer to have him think of cross-training. People did get sick and had accidents. And the women he employed might get pregnant.

I hope all my counseling doesn't turn me into an alcoholic.

Eleanor and I went to see Father Timothy. On the way there, she let me know her plans. Since she had many friends in Saltash and I was Baron here, it left a bit of a quandary.

She and Marian had decided that we would be wed at the mile marker between the two Baronies. That would allow people from both lands to attend.

I pictured a wedding in an open field. Since rain was always possible, I was proud to suggest erecting a large pavilion.

It was to be a large permanent pavilion similar to those over the Keep's well.

After the wedding, the pavilion could be used as a halfway resting point between Owen-nap and Saltash. In time it would grow to be a village.

Later she explained to Father Timothy that he and her town priest would officiate at the wedding. Splitting the difference would keep things smooth between the two towns.

Later as a group, we toured the school, still in session. The school day lasted from sunup until sun down five days a week.

William and Eleanor were impressed with our efforts and looked to do the same in Saltash. There was no question that we would be a local powerhouse when the two Baronies combined.

With my plans, we would be an island-wide powerhouse.

Supposedly we were still Roman Britannica, but the island was multiple countries with different levels of government. All owe allegiance to the governor in London, but that was only lip service in most cases.

At dinner that night in my temporary abode, a ragged group of four people was brought into our presence.

They looked on their last legs, so I had them seated and fed before anything else. As they ate, their story unfolded. They were from the Bodmin Barony.

Baron Bodmin had sold most of their food stocks to raise money for men at arms. The money had been sent out, and bandits ambushed the bearers on their way to Saltash.

To make matters worse, the Baron and his family suffered from a grippe and died. They were fortunate that it didn't spread beyond the family. Now they had no money, no food, and no leadership.

The people that came to me were the village headman, priest, blacksmith, and chief men at arms. There were only five men at arms in total.

They asked if I would become their Baron, feeding and protecting them.

If I didn't do this, almost three hundred people would die. Of course, I said yes. A brief ceremony followed this, where they all swore allegiance to me.

After the meal, I sent the emissaries to guest rooms to sleep. They had walked for two days straight without stopping to beg for aid.

After settling, I had a long night of my own, arranging for a wagon train of food and other supplies to leave as soon as possible.

While this was happening, Baron Saltash listened intently to my orders. When everything appeared to be set in motion, I asked him what I had missed.

"Nothing. You even thought of things like tents for your drivers. I would have let them sleep under their wagons."

Eleanor added, "Taking goats to provide milk for the babies is brilliant."

The Baron said, "The entire family dying from the grippe, and only the family, sounds suspicious."

"I will not have any bodies dug up to review the cause of death," I said.

"And let murderers go free?" He asked.

"Is it murder to kill those who are doing their best to kill you and your family?"

"But it is a Baron's right to do as he will with his Barony!"

"How do most Barons get their Barony?"

The old Baron looked at me like I was mad, "Why by force of arms."

"It looks like Baron Bodmin lost his through force of arms. The only difference is the winners don't want the power."

We both let it drop and agreed to disagree without saying anything.

In the morning we gave the relief column half a day's head start and toured the book bindery at the monastery. Abbot Luke was proud of how they solved the need for so many letter slugs.

Once more, the Baron looked at me with questions in his eyes but was enthusiastic about what was being done. When he was told about the local newspaper the monks had started, he wanted one for Saltash immediately.

He and Abbot had a spirited negotiation about starting a newspaper in Saltash. It resulted in the

Baron paying for a press and supplies of ink, paper, letter slugs, and housing for the newspaper.

The Abbott would provide the ink, paper, and letter slugs from his supplies. He would send four Monks to run the paper and live on the premises. They would act as printers and reporters, plus distribute the newspapers.

Every newspaper had to have a name. My suggestion of The Saltash Times was accepted as exceptionally well thought out.

I was brilliant. Or, more likely, everyone realized how powerful I had just become.

Accompanied by the Bodmin people, who I had loaned horses, we left to catch the relief group after lunch. We caught them by dinner time. The next morning, we rode ahead to check out the local situation for when our contingent arrived.

Chapter 26

When we arrived at Bodmin, things were bad. Few people were moving in the village, and they were emaciated.

At their Keep, a smaller version of my original Keep, two men at arms were sitting in the main hall. They were in better shape than the people in the village but not much.

"I need you two to start letting all the outlying farms know that food is coming," I said.

"Who are you to give us orders?"

"Baron Owen-nap and the Bodmin Barony is now mine."

The two looked like a team, one burly, the other like a weasel. From the man's look, the weasel thought of himself as the next Baron. We'd see if he was smart enough not to fight it.

He was a smart weasel and immediately got up and left the common room with his partner in tow. I asked one of my men at arms to follow them and ensure they were doing as asked.

Looking around the common room, I noticed blood on the floor. That needed to be cleaned up without any questions being asked.

I had to find out what happened without officially acknowledging it unless it was the weasel and friend. Murder was one thing, a revolt another. I could live with a revolt.

There wasn't much to see in this Keep. The Baron was either a miser or broke. A search of his rooms found him to be a miser. A bound chest sat in the corner of the room. When opened, it contained almost three thousand silver.

His miserly ways had killed him, his wife and children, and many of his people. I felt sorry for everyone but him.

I left a man at arms guarding the chest. Being left alone told me that the weasel and friend probably weren't the killers. If they were, they would have been after the money. Whoever did it wanted to shut down the Baron and his family and didn't care about anything else.

When I returned to the village, my relief column had arrived. The cook from my Keep provided a meal, and Agnes, the midwife now Nurse Agnes, started checking out those who were ill.

A huge pot was rounded up, and the cook started a stew. Normally she lets them simmer for hours. This one wouldn't last for an hour.

Agnes had tents set up and water set to boil. Lots of water. Two tents were to be delousing stations, one for men and one for women.

Soon people from farms near the village came pouring in. I had a couple of the larger villagers help Agnes separate the groups. It was a form of triage.

Those that were ill were sent in one direction. Those that looked near death's door from starvation were fed a small amount of bread and cheese.

Fortunately, while emaciated, most of the citizens weren't in dire straits.

Those that had no other problems were put in line for delousing. All of the people would need it before the day was done.

Eleanor became a strong assistant to Agnes. I was proud of how she stepped up without any prompting. Her father was helping Father Timothy set up a station to start a census.

A tour of the village granary revealed a bare interior. They had even eaten the seeds for this spring planting. What was the Baron thinking?

I dispatched a message back to Owen-nap requesting more food. I asked my lead farm supervisor to put together a team, bringing seeds, plows, and men to use them. The locals were in no shape to prepare the fields and plant them.

I also arranged for a road crew to start a proper road from Owen-nap to Bodmin. It would normally take a month to build the road, but I promised a bonus if it could be done in two weeks.

The road crews were getting good at their work. Slow at first, and they were now making miles a day. The road from Owen-nap to Wendon was complete.

Baron Saltash liked my roads so much that he asked me to train a crew from Saltash to build their roads. My road supervisor informed me that Saltash had sent four crews to be trained.

While the supervisor groused about following up on all the workers, I was thrilled. The training would be on the job. Not only would the roads to Saltash and Bodmin be completed this spring, but work on secondary roads to each farm area could be started.

I finally asked Baron Saltash something that had been bothering me.

"Do you owe fealty to anyone?"

"No, Cornwall is considered the wilds. Each Baron is his own Lord. Like the Scots in the north, we go our own way."

"Then our titles are self-awarded?" I asked.

"That is one way to put it."

"Since I now control a much larger area, I could award myself a higher title?"

"You could, but I don't recommend it."

"Why?"

"The other Barons surrounding you already are jealous of your success. If you declare a higher title, it would be as though you were claiming them."

I thought for a moment, "It was a passing thought. I'm not ready to take the war to the Barons."

Saltash gave me a long stare, "That sounds as though you might in the future."

"If needs be. We have to stop them from starving people every winter out of greed. If it takes war, then so be it."

The old Baron didn't respond.

And I changed the subject.

"After talking to John Steward, I'm leaving Sergeant Smith in charge here. He is a grizzled old warrior with no family."

The Baron looked up at that.

"Why is the no family important?" He asked.

"No wife to push for her child to be a Baron."

"He will have many women wanting to be his wife."

"His war wounds take care of that problem. He now has no interest in women except for a good meal," I said.

"He sounds perfect."

"There always will be problems, but this is the best I can do. It won't always be that easy."

The Baron chuckled, "You could send out recruiting parties."

I let out a great laugh at that. If I paid enough, some old soldier might have himself gelded. I think we will let that idea rest.

Another message was to Abbot Luke. I requested him to send out census teams as he did in Owen-nap and Wendon.

I asked the Bodmin village headman who the best farmers in the area were. He named a half dozen, and I asked him to summon them to me. I was going to send them to Owen-nap to see what had been accomplished. If they bought in, we could start four crop rotations this spring.

We would need more plows and associated equipment.

I wrote another message. This one to Thomas Smith. He was to increase the production of farming implements. At the same time, there was to be no lessening of crossbow production.

With that in mind, I asked John Billings, the Bodmin village headman, if there were ten unemployed young men that I could send to Owen-nap to be trained as men at arms. When I told him the pay rate, he told me he could have twenty men lined up in an hour.

I had Sergeant Smith pick out the ten to send. I had told Billings that they were to be men at arms. They would be trained on the crossbow, which was the easiest to learn. We needed firepower if we were attacked like I think we would be.

My messages were using up the old Baron's paper supply. He wasn't interested in communicating as he didn't have a lot of paper on hand.

I was down to writing on the back of older documents he had kept.

So far, I had sent three teenage boys at different times with messages to Owen-nap. I would soon be sending young ladies if it kept up.

I mistakenly shared that thought with Eleanor and the Baron at dinner that night. I meant it in jest. Eleanor took it seriously and informed me that young women were as capable as young men.

In later times, she would have been a suffragette or marched for women's rights. Instead of fighting for voting rights, she fought against women being considered property.

In my history, that battle had taken thousands of years. I wanted to speed that timeline up if possible.

I quickly let Eleanor know that I had been jesting. I knew women were as capable as men and, in some cases, more capable. She took this well, but I saw that some things weren't to be joked about. Fair enough.

The three of us talked into the night about the changes that had been made to Owen-nap and my plans for the future.

The food supply and production had increased, so fewer people were tied to the land. I was working to do away with serfdom by selling the land to the remaining farmers and then taxing them.

We debated the pros and cons of doing this. Both father and daughter finally agreed that everyone's standard of living would be better in the future. I had to explain the concept of standard of living.

Once they both understood the cycle of wealth created by everyone living better, they started talking about how it could be done in Saltash.

It took two more days before I was satisfied that I had done all I could to stabilize Bodmin and feed the people. Leaving Agnes and others behind to clean the place up and teach sanitation, we returned to Owen-nap.

I made certain that Eleanor knew that Nurse Agnes had been left with the work to do as she was most capable. The men at arms were hers to command. Woe unto those that didn't follow her 'advice.'

On the way back to my Keep, we passed roadcrews busy at work. It looked like I would be paying a bonus to all of them. I had to smile when I saw the road crew supervisor riding almost at a gallop between crews. No standing around on this project!

Back at Owen-nap, I was thrilled to see that the last section of the village wall had been poured and was now curing. Within a week, the village would be impregnable to local armies.

The walls of the Keep itself had been finished earlier and the interior work of the Keep was well in hand. I would be able to move back to my home soon.

Once more, I had to stop and think about what I now considered home.

The first night back, I learned something else about this culture I hadn't put together. Being engaged gave all the rights to marriage except the exchange of property.

Baron Saltash retired early, claiming fatigue. When Eleanor followed me to my room, I realized he didn't want to watch his daughter's steps toward womanhood.

I never talked about the bed chamber, but it was an amazing night.

The next day Eleanor, her maid, and Marian, the maid assigned to her, left to check on Father Timothy and the construction of the wedding pavilion.

In fear of bandits, I insisted that men at arms accompany the women. Eleanor fussed at this until she met the men at arms that I had chosen.

They were a mounted group of female auxiliaries who guarded the village and Keep when the men were at war.

As my precious rode away, I realized two things. I had just created the Baroness's Own. They would be her personal guard.

I also had to quit the Tolkien references! Especially any that included Eleanor and a Gollum. That was a quick way to the cold shoulder.

I spent the morning reviewing information from my spies in the other Baronies. Things had been going too well, and I was waiting for the other shoe to drop.

From the information gathered, the Barons of Pirthtowan and Wadebridge had discussed joining forces to attack me.

Based on that information, I had hidden scout camps at each border. Their orders were to have in place a huge wood pile to be kept undercover so that it wouldn't get wet. If the enemy crossed the border, they would light it off and ride for Owennap. Halfway there would be a second beacon. When the riders reached it, they would light the fire, giving us two warning beacons.

Thanks, Mr. Tolkien, for the signal fires.

These signals should give me time to assemble our forces.

John and I would ride out on the morrow and select our battle sites.

Chapter 27

John Steward and I were near the school when classes let out on the last day. The students came running out of the building, yelling about being out of school. A memory came back to me, and I chanted.

"School's out, school's out, the teacher let the monkeys out."

I thought I was clever in introducing this time-honored chant.

John asked me, "What's a monkey?"

Oh boy, I've done it now. As I thought that Father Timothy came walking out of the school with several teaching Monks.

"Father Timothy, I have a question for you," I said.

"Yes."

"Does the bible mention apes?"

I asked this, knowing full well they did.

"There are several passages where there is talk of ships from Tarshish bringing gold, silver, and apes."

"Do you know what an ape is?" I asked.

"I was taught that it is a manlike creature covered in hair. It is immensely strong but can't speak though there are signs of intelligence. They beat their chests and make a lot of noise."

He continued, "It is thought that when God created man, he made several attempts, and apes were an early failure. I find that hard to believe because God is all-powerful. He wouldn't have failures."

I took a chance, "Maybe they weren't failures. Maybe God hadn't made up his mind."

Father Timothy rubbed his chin.

"That will take some thought."

I turned to John, "The monkeys I referred to are like small apes."

He smiled, "So they beat their chests and make a lot of noise. Sounds like schoolchildren to me."

I then explained my chant to Father Timothy and the avidly listening Monks.

He and the Monks got a laugh out of it and repeated the chant several times to firmly plant it in their minds. It will be a dinner tale tonight at several tables.

I think I had just invented another saying and instituted a tradition that would last a long time.

Now that school was out the planting season was underway with a vengeance. I spent the next few days riding around Owen-nap, Bodmin, and Wendon to see that all was going as planned.

The farmers all greeted me cheerfully, especially in Bodmin. I had saved many of their lives and was now showing them a better way to live.

A census of Bodmin had been completed adding another four hundred and some souls to my domain. There were none with any special talents but many a strong back. Those strong backs were what we needed.

I often wondered when we would be attacked. I soon discovered there would be no attack, at least this year.

I wasn't the only one with spies. The Barons of Wadebridge and Pirthtowan realized that they couldn't conquer me with the walls around Owen-nap and my Keep. They were also now aware of my crossbow corps. They couldn't raise enough men to win, so they set aside any war plans for the year.

I wondered if I could make an alliance with them. The one thing I knew was that I couldn't afford any poor neighbors. Eventually, they would become jealous and cause problems.

That or all their people would flee those Baronies. Before that could go too far, there would be war as the Barons tried to hold on to their power.

The main roads connecting Bodmin, Wendon, Saltash, and Owen-nap had been completed by late spring. Now we could work on the internal networks of each Barony.

Owen-nap had most of its roads in place. Wendon was a close second. Bodmin barely started. Saltash Would be up to Baron Saltash. He was dragging his feet for some reason, but I didn't have time to go to Saltash to investigate.

The main roads were double-wide, with pull-offs laid out for large caravans. I had no doubt that some enterprising person would want to start a chain of inns.

I could have done it myself and made a small fortune, but I wanted to share the wealth as things were built. It would make a strong middle class that currently didn't exist.

A country was only strong when it had a vibrant, growing middle class. The rich had money but tended to keep it to themselves rather than invest it in their country. And they would always find ways to avoid taxes.

The middle class was the tax-paying class. There was more of the middle class so that the government would have more funding with a lesser amount from each.

Not that I wanted to protect the rich. I just had to find ways to make them want to invest rather than hoard their wealth.

In my press to bring my Barony into the industrial age, I had got ahead of myself. I have done this several times. My latest error was in starting the construction of water-powered bellows for a blast furnace.

The furnace would improve the production of pig iron many times over. I knew the plans to build the furnace and had the required materials. What I overlooked was having enough leather to make the huge bellows.

The current tanning process takes over a year to tan a hide. There were enough hides in the cold soaking process to make the bellows, but they wouldn't be available for a long time.

I always tried to lead people to find solutions themselves. But there was no reasonable way to do this, so I sat down with Simon Tanner over a mug of beer and described the process I had learned while I was unconscious. Instead of cold soaking for a year, he should try a salt bath. The tanning process could be completed in days rather than years.

I told him the amount of salt per gallon of water, then a gallon per pound of hide. He agreed to try it because it wouldn't take much effort. All I had to do was provide the salt.

Two days later, he was telling all that I was God Touched. I had changed a trade that had been constant forever. He had enough hides tanned to make my bellows.

If that had been my only problem, I would be happy as all get out. My next project was to build a Bessemer furnace to convert pig iron into steel. That wouldn't be a problem because, in my engineering studies, I read books on the processes of making steel in large quantities.

There was nothing needed that wasn't available in this day and age. Except for measuring instruments! Without micrometers and vernier calipers, mass production with interchangeable parts wouldn't be possible.

Another minor thing that drove me nuts for a while was my attempt at a metric system. The locals refused to use it!

They adopted my meter as a measure but promptly called it a long yard. They then divided it into feet and inches. Instead of kilograms, they became the Baron's pounds and ounces. Liters were small quarts. I finally gave in for several reasons.

One: my system was based on arbitrary units, which were best estimates of the true metric measures, and Two: I hated the metric system in my former life, why was I trying to impose it now?

So we used the common names for units based on my finger widths. Contrary to popular belief, the foot used didn't reflect any other body parts.

We could always use more high-carbon steel, so I continued with the Bessemer furnace project while working with the Monks to develop finer measurements.

We would be able to make items like rebar, but not interchangeable parts.

I started the Monks off with transversals. These grids were able to achieve an accuracy of one-hundredth of an inch. We needed verniers and micrometers to a thousandth to be of use.

A transversal would divide a hundredth to ten one-thousandths. The problem was that we had nothing that would accurately scribe the lines. The human eye couldn't consistently see that fine, and the blades we had were too wide.

We needed a true microscope to see the subdivisions. Water worked well for demonstrating bacteria, but we need glass lenses for this. We could make a clear glass but grinding it to the correct shape was another story.

From my funny memory, I was able to draw a diagram of the shapes needed for magnification, but achieving that shape was a different story. That would require days of hand polishing with iron oxide, which we had plenty of.

We didn't have boron oxide, sodium carbonate, or zinc oxide. And without these, we couldn't make optical-grade glass. Until we had trade established with Italy, Turkey, and China, we were stuck making things to one-hundredth of an inch and then hand-working them to fit.

This method was better than what we had before but didn't lend itself to mass production.

My backup plan was to cold stamp as many parts as possible. The stamping dies would have to be hand worked so the parts would be interchangeable, but once the dies were made, we could produce them in large quantities. Large for this time, not millions, still the thousand made before too much die wear would be adequate.

Hot stamping would be more difficult to achieve as it required combining preheating metal and cooling the dies, which was complicated.

I was considering these problems when I realized another event took precedence. My wedding.

I had been viewing the wedding itself taking place in some distant future. Well, here in the spring of 717, the time had arrived. I had studiously avoided the border between Saltash and Owen-nap, so I hadn't seen the pavilion that had been built.

My only participation was to stand still while a seamstress from Saltash and her assistants measured me for a suit and the later fitting.

The day before the wedding, John Steward escorted me to a newly built house near the border. I would spend the night here. The reasoning was severalfold. It would ensure I would be at the altar on time, sober, and clean.

As we ate a quiet meal that evening, I asked John,

"You don't have bachelor parties?"

"What's a bachelor party?"

Here we go again!

"In some places, it is a tradition that on the night before the wedding, the groom and his groomsmen would have a wild party to celebrate the last night of freedom from the wedded state."

"Why would the stablemen have a party and not the soon-to-be wedded man?"

I must have looked like a fish as I worked my mouth. That is until John burst out laughing.

"Normally, we do, but Lady Eleanor gave us strict instructions."

I pretended to grump, but the thought of having a hangover on my wedding day wasn't pleasant. I could act put upon while not having a headache.

The wedding day was bright and clear, with no sign of rain in sight. John and I had a simple breakfast prepared by a lady who arrived at daybreak.

I had time to wash in the warm water heated on the stove. After dressing in my new finery, we rode to the pavilion.

We were to arrive at precisely ten o'clock. Since we didn't have clocks, it was by the sun's height over the horizon, but our orders were clear. Be there on time!

Taking no chances, we arrived at the edge of the border early. There was a huge crowd at the border.

It was like the first day of school or a market square. I looked for a t-shirt vendor, but that tradition hadn't appeared yet. Maybe I should have it suggested to some widows and orphans trying to make ends meet.

The crowd was so thick that it took time to make it to the pavilion. This entrance brought us to the front of the pavilion door, where we stopped. This was different from what I was used to, but women had been working on achieving the perfect wedding for thousands of years. Perfection would be an ever-moving goal.

Chapter 28

On time and in place for the wedding, I was dressed like a popinjay. Needless to say, I had no choice of what to wear. My bride and her maids selected my clothing.

John Steward, my best man, Tom Smith, and Mark Woodson, my groomsmen, and I were waiting inside the door of my changing cottage for our signal to exit.

John asked, "How did she get you to wear this outfit?"

"She just showed it to me and told me it was what I was wearing to the wedding."

"You didn't argue or outright refuse?"

"Have you heard of 'happy wife, happy life'?"

They hadn't and thought it was the funniest thing they had ever heard. They each repeated it several times so they wouldn't forget it.

"Where do you get these sayings?" Mark asked.

"I don't know. I have always known."

"Are there any others we should know?"

"Yes, dear. You're right. I'm wrong. I'm sorry."

It is a wonder they weren't rolling on the ground on that one. Tears came to Mark and Tom's eyes. John, the single man in the crowd, laughed, but you could tell he was puzzled.

John asked, "Why is that so funny?"

Tom told him, "You have to be married to understand. With that statement, you end the argument and give the win to your wife. There is nothing she can say after that without being a harpy. At the same time, how you say it tells her you don't care enough to argue. That makes her angrier, but she can't say anything."

I butted in, "That works several times; after that, she will ignore it and continue, so choose wisely when using it, no more than twice a year."

"My Lord, how did you get so wise," asked Mark.

"I must be God Touched!"

This statement brought more laughter. It came to a halt when Father Timothy opened the door for us to exit. It was time.

I was calm and nervous at the same time. I couldn't explain my feelings for anything.

We were joining the wedding procession. I was told this was the latest fashion in weddings in London.

The wedding procession began with minstrels playing various instruments, including bagpipes, the six-stringed viol, flutes, drums, and trumpets.

Our minstrels had been imported from London by Baron Saltash at his daughter's request. This group previously had been the servants of royals and nobles but broke away from the courts. As traveling troubadours, they provided entertainment and music to all who would listen.

Later, when I learned what they had been paid, I understood why they had gone independent.

Following the musicians, Eleanor and I walked toward the church. She walked on my left side since God fashioned Eve out of Adam's left rib.

Directly behind us rode the best man, John, on horseback. Outfitted with his sword, I chose him for his skills as a swordsman, he was the best swordsman.

He rode along to protect us from harm. We might fall prey to kidnappers. Also, such a display of wealth might attract the wrong kind of attention. Furthermore, despite the posting of the bans, some nefarious parties might attempt to put a stop to the wedding.

Tomas walked behind as another guard. It was because his huge arms could handle the biggest broadsword I had ever seen. It must have been seven feet long. One swing would cleave a man in two.

Following just behind the best man, John was Baron Saltash. Eleanor's mother was deceased, as were my parents. John was standing in for them. In fact, John had raised the real Baron.

Upon arriving at the church/pavilion, the minstrels ceased playing, and those attending the bride and groom lined up quietly outside the church doors.

Eleanor's priest, holding the wedding ring, and Father Timothy stood just before the closed doors beneath the portico.

When all fell silent, the priest opened the proceedings with a series of important questions.

How old are the bride and groom?

Are the bride and groom related to each other by blood?

Does the bride's father permit the marriage?

Were the bans published properly?

Do both the bride and the groom consent freely to enter into marriage?

After we answered appropriately to all these questions, Father Timothy read aloud the dowry agreement. Finally, I offered the bride a coin purse with 13 coins. After the ceremony, Eleanor would disburse the coins to the poor as a sign of her authority to make financial decisions in my name.

At this point, Baron Saltash encouraged his daughter to take her place in front of the priest. Meanwhile, Thomas escorted me to stand beside the bride. Again, the bride stood to the left side of the groom as we faced the priest.

I then plighted my wedding vows. I promised "to have and to hold" my bride in bed and at the table, whether she be fair or ugly, for better or worse, in sickness and in health, to death us do part."

Eleanor offered no vows, remaining silent throughout the proceedings. Following my vows, the priest offered a short homily on the sacred act of marriage. Then he blessed the wedding ring and handed it to me. So where does the obey part come in?

As I slid the wedding ring on and off the bride's first, second, and third fingers, I recited the "In the name of the Father, and of the Son, and of the Holy Ghost, with this ring, I thee wed."

Finally, Father Timothy opened the church doors and ushered Eleanor, me, our attendants, and the best man to the altar. Everyone else took their seats among the other guests.

We knelt before the priest at the altar. The attendants held a canopy over our heads while Eleanor's priest said mass. Upon the conclusion of mass, the attendants removed the canopy.

The priest then bestowed upon me a kiss of peace. I, in turn, bestowed the kiss of peace upon Eleanor. The priest then closed the wedding with a blessing. As we walked out of the church, the choir chanted Agnus Dei.

On the way out, it hit me. I was married again. I glanced at the beautiful vibrant young woman next to me in wonder.

When I first appeared in this time, my goal was survival. Then it was to improve life for my people. Now I had a wife, and I wanted to take care of her and make her life as good as possible.

That was now. In the future, there probably will be children. I had to build a better world for them.

Dory and I had always been a team. I wanted that with Eleanor. Better yet, a full partner. Dory always supported me in my endeavors, but because of the nature of the military, she couldn't be a full partner. But Eleanor could. I would include her in all important decisions of my rule.

Eleanor must have read my mind because she sighed and leaned into me.

"I have wonderful news, husband."

"What is that?"

"I'm pregnant."

That was not what I thought.

The crowd must have thought me mad at my shout of jubilation. I then picked Eleanor up in a princess carry and almost ran to our table in the pavilion.

We had been intimate for the last six weeks, so it was no surprise, yet it was. Now I have a true goal in my new life.

From the smirks on Marian's and Ann's faces, they knew. Baron Saltash had a surprised but knowing look. John was confused.

"Eleanor and I have a child!"

This was not the Middle Ages, where every bride was expected to be a virgin. It was the exact opposite. Proof of fertility was considered to be a sign of good luck and a healthy marriage.

None of that namby-pamby blood on the bed sheet, white wedding dress, or witnessing the act here.

We were healthy young animals and proved we could go forth and multiply, as stated in the bible.

Those close by repeated it to others so that all present knew. Cheers went up as the word spread.

Now people came up to congratulate us. Even the Barons from Pirthtowan and Wadebridge had come when invited.

The two Barons asked if they could have a private word later. We agreed that we would meet after the noon meal the next day. Our wedding celebration was to last for three days.

We feasted and danced all day. That night Eleanor and I slept together in the little cottage I had changed in. This small building will always be special to me.

The next morning started very slowly for everyone present. Most had slept on the benches in the pavilion. Some, like the Barons, had large tents erected.

There must have been five hundred people at the wedding, and all had stayed overnight. This morning Eleanor demonstrated her powers of planning. Privies had been dug, and temporary kitchens were in place to feed all. A new well had even been dug to ensure a safe water supply. These details all had come under the heading of wedding preparations. Most brides were worried about table seating and the paper used for the invitation. She built a small city.

Men at arms took a day each to keep the peace. There were bound to be disagreements with five hundred present, all drinking. That was when I found out she even had a drunk tank built.

It had four sections. These were to separate men and women and those in conflict from each other.

After the prisoners slept it off, they were released. Second offenders were kept for the duration, and a Monk was keeping a record. If nothing else, we were identifying future troublemakers.

The more I saw, the more I was impressed with my new wife.

There was talk of the dowry, which had been announced at the church steps. Normally there would be coins and land at this level of nobility.

Baron Saltash instead gave Eleanor and me his Barony! He would be retired but would act as an advisor in need.

This was more than generous. He was surrendering all of his power. I would now be Baron Saltash-Owen-nap. Some had been referring to me as

Baron Bodmin-Owen-Nap. Would it now be Baron Saltash-Owen-nap-Bodmin?

"William, why have you done this? I thought the negotiated dowry was excessive, but this goes beyond," I said.

"It solves a problem for me."

"What is that?"

"There is this woman."

Since he was always in the company of the widow Catherine, it wasn't a mystery who the woman was.

Eleanor spoke up, "It's about time, father!"

The Baron continued, "She is young enough that we might still have children. By giving up the title, there is no question of the succession."

He signaled to Lady Catherine, who had been sitting close by. Both Eleanor and I wished her well in her soon-to-be marriage. She wasn't a Lady yet but would be when she wedded the Baron.

Catherine was a plump little handful, as the Baron described her. She blushed as he told us that. Dark-haired, with bright eyes and fair of face, I could see what he saw in her. The large breasts and wide hips didn't hurt.

After our luncheon, Eleanor and I met with the two Barons.

They surprised me to no end. First, there was the title confusion. We had a good laugh as we tried various combinations. Baron Wadebridge suggested I adopt 'Baron of the Middle Counties'.

This name made such sense that after gaining Eleanor's opinion, that was what it would be. Our banner would be a quartering of each of the three Baronies I now owned, along with a new symbol for the new title.

After the name was out of the way, I asked.

"My lords, why have you asked for this meeting?"

"We would like to join you in an alliance."

Eleanor and I had discussed why the Barons had requested a meeting the night before. This was our first guess, and we had decided on our answer.

"That is excellent news, My Lords."

I didn't question them on the why. I knew why. They couldn't conquer me, so they wanted to join me. That was fine.

"Eleanor and I are all for it. Now, what would this alliance comprise? As it is said, the Devil is in the details."

This statement put them on notice that Eleanor and I were in on it together. What I didn't realize was that I was introducing a new phrase.

Even Eleanor had never heard me say that, so we had to discuss what it meant. The three of them quickly caught on, and we spent the next two hours hammering out a deal.

Chapter 29

The Barons had a proposal for our alliance. It was straightforward. We would improve the roads throughout their Baronies at my cost. We would also share and implement all our farming knowledge for them during the first season.

As far as mutual defense went, I was to send all my troops if they were involved in a war with another Barony. This pact included them instigating the war.

They promised some undefined aid to me if I was invaded by another Barony. The kicker was that they were the only ones in position to attack Owen-nap.

I was speechless when I first heard this proposal. Then I burst out into laughter.

"You must be kidding. That is the most one-sided proposal I have ever heard."

Baron Pirthtowan asked, "Do you have a counter?"

"Yes, I will return home, and you can approach me when you have a reasonable proposal."

The Baron replied, "That isn't bargaining in good faith, Owen-nap."

I chose to ignore the lesser title used.

"When I'm presented with a good faith proposal, I will respond."

Pirthtowan came back with, "We will give you time to reconsider your lack of cooperation. When you are ready, contact us."

Eleanor had been sitting beside me during the talk. I wouldn't refer to it as a negotiation.

"What do you think, Eleanor?"

"I think they are trying to come up with a reason to go to war with you, but at the same time, they are afraid of your power."

"I think you are right."

She continued, "We can test them by presenting a reasonable counterproposal."

We returned to our primary home at Owen-nap. Saltash would be our second home. We would visit Bodmin when needed but not make it a home.

The next several weeks were spent reviewing our operations.

The mills were now all in production. Even the new blast furnace had its first pours. The mines were producing more than current needs and creating stockpiles of lime, coal, and iron ore.

We would use these stockpiles up after the growing and harvesting seasons. We had a backlog of roads, housing, and walls around the villages that needed construction.

The extra labor during the summer was being used to dig wells, create safe cesspools, redirect streams, and dam them for ponds for later mill construction.

The crops had come in well. If nature cooperated, we would have a bumper crop.

Crews were working on the infrastructure at Bodmin as they were in the worst shape. They didn't even have a usable grain storage silo. The one they had wasn't water or rodent proof. It's a wonder they hadn't starved a long time ago.

Two weeks after our meeting with the Barons Pirthtowan and Wadebridge, I sent them a message with a counterproposal. Eleanor, John Steward, and I had spent some hours on it.

Its basics were that I would build roads to their borders at my expense. I would let them hire my men and equipment to build them within their borders.

They could send farmers to observe our methods for free but would have to buy equipment from us.

If another Barony directly attacked them, I would send some forces to help. The numbers sent would depend on the attackers. If I was attacked, I expected the same.

There was even a list of costs for them to consider. The prices were reasonable, but we had left some room for negotiation.

Weeks went by with no response. I wondered what they might be up to.

In the meantime, crops were ripening, and everyone was getting ready for the fall harvest.

I hadn't been to Saltash in a while, so I planned a trip to the port. Eleanor was going through a queasy stage of her pregnancy, so she was staying home. Riding in the carriage all day would leave her motion sick.

I didn't want to ride in the carriage, but my new status demanded that I do so. I was saved by the Dowager Baroness Wendon, who asked if she could join us so she and her son could visit her father.

I graciously gave up the carriage to them and would ride horseback all the way. I was jubilant because the coach wasn't sprung, and it was a hard ride, even on our improved roads. I made a mental note to show Tom Smith leaf springs and suspension arrangements.

It was a pleasant day when we started out, but a weather system moved in and soaked all but those in the coach. Maybe I had made the wrong choice.

We had a scout out front of our small procession and ten men at arms with the new crossbows were accompanying me. The new bows were about one-third the size of the battle ones, designed for close in defense.

Each man carried two of them, cocked and locked. With the steel bow strings, dampness or weakening over time was not an issue. My small force could take on a much larger one.

Then there were two coachmen, plus several Monks on various errands.

We were all alert as the forest hadn't been cut back from the road as much as I had planned. I would have to find out why when we got back to Owen-nap. In the meantime, it was a spot ripe for an ambush.

The scout came riding back to report that a small stream ahead was above its banks. It was so small in its normal flow that a bridge hadn't been built.

The scout reported he thought it would be okay. The use of okay had spread.

I wanted to see for myself, as we would have to make camp early if the stream was too high. So, I rode a mile to the stream with the scout to see if the crossing was safe.

Once there, I agreed with the scout that we could still ford the stream. Halfway back to our group, I heard metal on metal and both men and horses screaming. I kicked my horse into a gallop, thinking it must be bandits.

As I got closer, I saw that a small battle was just finishing up. It looked like three of my men, and about twenty bandits were down.

Then I realized that the coachmen were not on their perch. Looking closer, they were on the ground, dead.

Arriving and dismounting at a jump. I ran to the coach's right-side door. When I opened it, there was a grim sight. The Dowager Baroness and her son were dead with several arrows in them.

The opposite door was open, and I saw a man running away. He hadn't got far.

The sergeant accompanying me rode up, and I told him, "Capture that man, alive if possible."

The sergeant took off with two troopers following him. I thought of them as cavalry troopers though they called themselves men at arms on foot or on horseback.

I wondered what they would be called when I invented airplanes. The mind goes to strange places under stress.

Examining the Dowager Baroness and her son made it clear they were dead. We had lost them, the two coachmen, three men at arms, and one Monk.

The bandits left twenty dead on the field and at least one on the loose. We had finished loading our dead in the carriage and stripped the dead bandits of their belongings.

Each bandit had a purse on them with twenty new silver pieces in them. This was more than simple banditry.

The sergeant and two men at arms returned with the prisoner alive. A search revealed he had fifty silver on him. We had captured the leader.

He was a hard-bitten man who had been through many battles.

"It is obvious that you and your men aren't simple bandits. They are all dead, and you will be soon. I'll give you a choice. Tell me who hired you, and it will be quick. If you don't tell me, you will be tortured until you do, then killed. What is your choice?"

He looked at me for what seemed like forever. I was about to tell him it was torture when he spoke up.

'I can see from your eyes that you will do it. Since I'm a dead man, I will tell you."

"Who hired you?"

"The Barons of Pirthtowan and Wadebridge."

"Why did you kill the Dowager and her son?"

"We were told you would ride in the coach, so I told my men to kill everyone inside it."

"Is there anyone to be told of your death?" I asked.

"No one. This band was the last of my mercenaries. We had fallen into hard times and took this job out of desperation. I have no family."

"Make your peace with the Lord."

As he closed his eyes, I nodded to the Sergeant, who was carrying a war hammer. He brought it down on the mercenary's head, killing him with one blow.

"Drag all the bodies into the woods and dig a shallow grave. It will take time for news of their failure to get back to the Barons."

It took the rest of the day to clean up the ambush site and bury the bodies. We made camp there and left at first light. We now had twenty-five extra horses that had belonged to the mercenaries.

Arriving in Saltash, I had a terrible chore. I had to tell John Chandler that his daughter and grandson were dead.

The man was made of iron. He showed no emotion as I informed him of their deaths and the end of the mercenary company. He directed two servants to bring the bodies into the house.

"Thank you for returning them. I will make their funeral arrangements. And thank you once more for bringing those responsible to justice," he said.

"They were the killers. Those responsible are about to see my justice."

At that, the iron man gave way to a grieving parent. I held him as he cried. It wasn't long, but the depths of his sobs were chest-racking.

When he had settled down, he gave me directions to the church where I could have my people interred. It was too warm to even think of taking them back to Owen-nap.

That errand completed, I went to the Saltash keep, my keep now. William and his soon-to-be bride were still in residence. I brought them up to date on events.

He told me, "I recommend taking twenty men at arms from here when you leave."

"Thank you, I intend to take the battle to them as soon as possible. I don't want to give them time to prepare."

"What are your immediate plans?" He asked.

"To send two riders with extra horses back to Owennap to have Eleanor pull together all my men at arms along with a supply train. She will also notify Wendon and Bodmin of events, but I will leave their forces there.

"With the twenty from here, I will have sixty men at arms. All of mine will have crossbows. The two Barons only have thirty men between them, so we should make this quick."

I then penned a note to Eleanor explaining what was needed. I also verbally gave it to both riders. They left within the hour of my meeting with William.

I followed them with the additional men at arms the next morning. We each had an extra horse, and I left the cursed coach with Saltash. I told him to burn or sell it, no matter to me.

We made it back to Owen-nap by that evening. The horses were exhausted, but we made it.

Upon arrival, Eleanor had a late dinner arranged. While we ate, she updated me on events.

"The men have been assembled, and the supply train will be loaded and ready to leave in the morning."

"Thank you, dear, and how are you doing?"

"The morning sickness is still with me, but it is getting better. Agnes is closely monitoring me and has a midwife in training following me everywhere I go."

That explained the young lady sitting in the corner.

"Everywhere?"

"Not our bed chamber tonight."

"Good."

Chapter 30

At what we called o'dark thirty in the army, my small squad left town. We were on our way to Pirthtowan first, as it was the closest, and their roads were in better shape.

Since we had killed the entire band of mercenaries, there was a chance we could take them by surprise. It should be an easy victory, even without surprise, unless they had prepared for failure and fortified their keep.

I didn't want to voice that thought. As sure as Murphy was alive and well, it would jinx us. My uptime British friends also had Sod's Law, which stated that Murphy was an optimist.

I had started using up time to think of my origin time. I had played with an alternate universe future and several other phrases trying to describe the situation. I ended up with uptime even though it might be uptime and sideways.

When the first dawn light appeared, I had just finished my coffee in a leather-covered mug and could see a rider approaching. It was a scout who had left even earlier than we had. He reported the road was clear to our border.

Two other scouts had left with him. They would advance to Pirthtowan. At the town's edge, one would return and let us know if any troops were out and about. The other would dismount and walk into the small village to see the condition of the fortress.

The scout would hide their horse in a small copse and hope it wouldn't be found in the short time they would be gone. He had a lute with him which he could play somewhat and pretend to be a wandering bard if questioned.

I heard a sample of his playing and hoped he wouldn't have any requests as they would run him out of town or worse. If questioned about me, he would say I hadn't returned to Owen-nap the night before, and a party was setting out to look for me.

His excuse for being in town so early was that he couldn't get any work in my Barony and was broke, so he left in the evening and had slept rough last night.

Of course, if the scouts ran into trouble, they were to return immediately.

The second scout returned to Pirthtowan territory and reported the road ahead was clear. Three hours later, we were close to the village when the third scout came riding up.

"My lord, the village has just stirred to a normal workday, the Keep's gates are wide open, and the guard on duty was still asleep when I left. I could have taken this place by myself."

"I thank you for leaving something for us to do."

We both laughed.

I had deliberately made a joke of it. From my previous combat experience leading troops in World War II, it was good to hear their leader was confident.

I don't know why that worked with bullets flying all around as we built a bridge or mined a tank trap. For myself, I knew I was faking, I was scared shitless.

Looking back, I knew it worked with me when my Captain would arrive in his jeep and give us another dangerous assignment while making an off-the-wall joke. I wondered if Roosevelt had made bad jokes to Eisenhower on D-day.

The scout's report was accurate. When we marched through Pirthtowan village, the residents ran for their houses. There was no resistance.

The guard had woken up at the keep gates but stood in amazement as we marched through. There wasn't any resistance until we reached the first door into the keep.

First out of the Keep's main door were the Baron's men at arms and Knights. They apparently were eating their first meal of the day when we arrived. Some were armed, most not. They were brave but foolish. My crossbowmen turned them into pincushions.

The Baron and his two adult sons followed. They had taken the time to get ready for battle but were cut down with crossbow bolts within seconds. The Keep was ours. Pirthtowan had fallen.

The Baron's wife had died, and he never remarried, so I didn't worry about claimants to the Barony in future years. I hated the thought of having to kill small children because, later, they could become symbols in a civil war.

It was common practice to do away with any that might prove to be a problem. Not that my twentieth-century upbringing wouldn't allow me to do that.

The Baron's two adult sons had stood and died with him so there wouldn't be problems in the future.

Wadebridge would be another story. From my spying, I knew the Baron had a young wife and children ranging in age from two to eight.

That was tomorrow's problem. Today I had to consolidate control of Pirthtowan. My first step was to have the village headman brought to me. He was the only one with authority left here.

"Your Baron, along with Wadebridge, attacked me and has paid the price. This Barony is now in my possession."

"Yes, My Lord."

"I'm leaving a small force here to keep the peace. My men and I will proceed to Wadebridge in the morning."

"Yes, My Lord."

"Send word to all outlying farms what has occurred."

"Yes, My Lord."

"Sergeant Tillman here will be in charge in my absence."

"Yes, My Lord."

I think this guy might be a yes-man.

While I was giving these instructions, Sergeant Tillman saw to the looting of the dead and arranging for their burial.

I rejoined my men as we searched the Keep. The place was a pigsty with no woman's touch to be seen. The Baron kept his money chest under his bed. Sergeant Tillman opened it with the key he had retrieved from the Baron's body.

From the ease with which the chest was dragged out from under the bed, I knew there wouldn't be much in it. There were only four hundred silver. No wonder the guy attacked us.

Pirthtowan was the third Barony that I had taken over. A routine was being developed. The monk-scribe that now accompanied me had a checklist of things to do. He had developed it on his own.

Thaddeus or Thad had been assigned to me as my scribe. The tall, thin, gangly boy was a treasure. He not only took notes for me but also tried to anticipate what was needed from those notes.

It made my life a lot easier not to have to tell people to check the food supply and ensure the food bins are rodent and waterproof. Or look at how waste disposal is handled and make corrections as needed.

All these things were now becoming routine. Thad would let John Steward know what needed to be done, and John would assign work crews.

Improvements that had taken months at first were now measured in weeks. Agnes, with her crew of nurses, would come to Pirthtowan to check everyone out. The census monks would do their thing. From being a one-man show, I had the beginnings of an organization.

While Thad was preparing orders for my signature, I reviewed the scouting report for the route from Pirthtowan to Wadebridge. Part of my spy's duties was to check out the roads, creeks, and rivers between major locations.

I had not planned to invade these Baronies, but I used the lessons I learned at the Pentagon. I had plans for all eventualities. The plans would change, but it would be easier if you had a framework.

I had participated in a planning session to invade Canada. It was weird but informative. I think assignments like that were given to all new personnel to get used to the idea of planning for anything.

We had surprise on our side with Pirthtowan. Wadebridge knew we would be coming by now.

The spy's report included a narrow bridge crossing a fast-running stream. This chokepoint would be a good spot for Baron Wadebridge to set up.

The Baron had approximately twenty men at arms and Knights. Most concerning was that the men at arms were trained with bows. Not the longbows of the future, but powerful enough to stand off from that bridge and make the crossing difficult.

I would have thirty-some troops. The Baron had twenty. These numbers weren't a good ratio for attacking a defended point. I should have had three times as many troops as he did.

The notes included a ford about a mile upstream from the bridge. I had a scout dispatched at first light to check that area out. If the Baron failed to defend that crossing, they were doomed.

By noon that day, we were almost to the bridge. The scout was waiting for us. Baron Wadebridge was on the other side of the bridge with his archers in position. We were in luck. The ford wasn't defended.

Ten men were detailed to the bridge. They were to remain out of sight until they heard the blast of a horn. It tickled my fancy that a ram's horn was being used. It seemed biblical. When the small force heard the horn, they would advance to the bridge and let themselves be seen.

They were to remain out of bow shot. The mission was to pin the defenders in place. Just as we couldn't cross the bridge, the Baron's men were stuck on their side. The ratio was now in our favor.

I led the other twenty men to the ford for a flanking action. Once we had crossed the ford and were halfway back to the bridge on the Wadebridge side, I had the horn sounded.

We took the Baron's troop by total surprise.

It was a slaughter. I was almost sickened by it. During my uptime wars, I was used to desperate fights. This fight was anything but. Other than wanting to throw up, this was a better way to do things, at least from my point of view.

The Baron had fallen in the fight. It looked like two of his men were able to flee. They would warn the Keep and the village.

Since there would be few troops, if any, at the Keep, I left five men to clean up the battlefield and marched to Wadebridge. On the way, I made the decision that I wouldn't kill the Baroness or her children. I didn't have it in me. Somehow, I would work it out.

The villagers were hiding in their homes or had fled to the fields. The gates to the Keep were wide open, and it was in better shape than any of the others I had conquered. They had a wall that could have been defended by the Baron's men.

They didn't have a well within the Keep's walls, so that it couldn't withstand a siege.

The Baroness made her own decision. Rather than be captured and killed, she killed her children with poison and then stabbed herself. I was sickened by these deaths. Needless and cruel, things had to change in this day and age.

Once more, Thad proved his usefulness in setting things in motion. It was a good thing because I was stunned not only by the Baroness killing her children but all the events of the last two years.

I had died and came back as a young Baron. I was now married with a child on the way, and the five baronies that surround Owen-nap were now under my control.

I had the beginnings of the infrastructure needed to start an industrial revolution. With a calorie surplus, we could shift to manufacturing. Though there remained the problem of being able to measure to one-thousandth of an inch so we could have parts interchangeability.

There was also the problem of training a workforce in using precision tools, jigs, fixtures, and measuring equipment.

With the five Baronies, I now had almost four thousand people in my domain. This population gave me a significant workforce.

My next big project was to open trade routes.

After spending two days bringing the Wadebridge Barony under my control, I returned home to Eleanor and our unborn child.

The next few years should be exciting.

End of Book 1 in the series

Backmatter

Next:

Cast in Time Book 2 Baron of the Middle Counties.

See more by Ed Nelson at enelsonauthor.com

Made in the USA
Middletown, DE
11 September 2023

38317972R00195